A Southern Quilting Cozy Christmas

A Southern Quilting Mystery, Volume 20

Elizabeth Craig

Published by Elizabeth Spann Craig, 2024.

A SOUTHERN QUILTING COZY CHRISTMAS

First edition. October 15, 2024.

Written by Elizabeth Craig.

Chapter One

Beatrice decided it couldn't get any cozier than this. She and Wyatt were together on their sofa, hot chocolates in hand, a corgi napping across their laps, Christmas music playing, and a fire crackling in the fireplace. Their Christmas tree was a Frasier fir from a local tree farm. Its fresh pine scent mingled with the woodsmoke from the fireplace. If you added in the snow flurries that were dancing across the windows, it made everything practically perfect.

The only problem, reflected Beatrice, was that so often when things seemed practically perfect, they took a dramatic turn in the wrong direction. This is precisely what happened when there was a peremptory knock at their front door. Noo-noo, the formerly-dozing corgi, woke with a start, barking frantically and looking quite embarrassed to be caught napping.

Wyatt put his hot chocolate down on the coffee table and made his way to the front door. "I hope everything's okay," he said.

Wyatt was the minister at the Presbyterian church just down the road from them. In his profession, it wasn't too unusual for unexpected phone calls or knocks on the door. Beatrice reluctantly stood to greet whoever was there.

It turned out it was Meadow from next door, and she was decidedly not facing any sort of genuine emergency whatsoever. Although she seemed to think she was.

"Beatrice!" she said. "I'm in a tizzy. My head is spinning with all the Christmas craft show details."

Wyatt was always kind and welcoming. Beatrice's patience was a work-in-progress. Perhaps she would make it a priority with a New Year resolution. So, while Beatrice was giving Meadow a tight smile, Wyatt was offering her hot chocolate and a place in front of the fire.

Meadow beamed at Wyatt. "You're the best! Yes, some hot chocolate would be wonderful. I can't remember the last time we saw snow flurries in mid-December. They're rather pretty, but I'm starting to feel like I was trapped in a snow globe."

"You walked over here?" asked Beatrice. She joined Meadow on the sofa.

"I sure did. I thought a short walk would help me clear my head. Boy, that was a mistake."

Beatrice said, "That's too bad. When I walk, it usually helps me get clarity on whatever is on my mind."

Meadow snorted. "Apparently, I have so much on my mind that my brain was overloaded and just crashed. But seriously, Beatrice, you should hear what I've got going on."

Beatrice had a fair idea what Meadow was grappling with. That's because it had been a topic on the agenda of the last several Village Quilter guild meetings she'd attended. It was, in fact, the precise reason she wasn't involved in planning the event.

Now it appeared she might be a sounding board for Meadow, which practically made her a planner by proxy.

"I thought the town of Dappled Hills was primarily responsible for organizing and putting on the craft fair," said Beatrice.

"They are. But somehow, I got dragged deeper and deeper into the crux of it all. The quilting displays and sales, the bake sale, the dog booth . . . it's all so very complex."

Wyatt returned with Meadow's hot chocolate. Meadow glanced around her and had the grace to look very slightly embarrassed. "Uh-oh. It looks like I just inserted myself in the middle of your nice, romantic evening."

Wyatt gave her a smile. "Not romantic, just quiet."

But it *could* have become romantic, thought Beatrice, suppressing a sigh. If someone hadn't arrived at the door.

Meadow said, "Anyway, I was hoping to settle myself down by telling you all about the craft show. A brain dump! Isn't that what they call it? Then I can be sedate when we go to the Christmas party tonight. You're both still going, aren't you?"

Beatrice thought, rather uncharitably, that the only way Meadow would become sedate is if she were given a sedative. "I'm going, yes. Wyatt is going to stay home tonight. He's had a busy week at the church, and he'll need to be up early for the Sunday service."

Wyatt's brow furrowed. "I could go, though. If you needed me there."

Meadow waved her hand dismissively. "No, no. You should stay here and relax. All of Beatrice's friends will be there. It's not like she'll be a wallflower. Now, where was I? Oh yes, the craft show."

Wyatt, bless him, was in full pastoral mode. "Is everything going all right with the show? Has taking it on been stressful?"

"Yes! It has been too stressful. So the next time I offer to be on any sort of committee, you two should stop me right away. Immediately."

Which was impossible in itself. Trying to stop Meadow from doing something was like trying to stop the tide with a broom.

"What kinds of things have you been up against?" asked Wyatt sympathetically.

Beatrice winced. Now they'd be in for it.

Sure enough, Meadow launched into a monologue involving vendor coordination, the curation of quilting displays, bake sale logistics, Santa's schedule for the dog booth, weather contingencies, and parking. Wyatt nodded sympathetically, while Beatrice gave Meadow a tight smile.

Finally, Meadow finished her soliloquy. "Whew!" she said. "Boy, do I feel better. It's nice getting all that stuff off my chest. When I try to tell Ramsay about the craft show madness, it's almost as if he's not really listening to me."

"Glad you feel better," said Beatrice. Although she suddenly felt rather stressed out herself.

Meadow stood up. "Now I'd better scramble back home. I've got to get Ramsay's supper together before the party or else he'll make himself sugary cereal and mess up all the good progress we've been making on his weight-loss." She looked at her watch. "I'll pick you up for the party, Beatrice. We're right next door to each other, after all, and I'm picking Miss Sissy up, too."

Miss Sissy was an elderly, irascible quilter. A woman of few words, but the few words were invariably spoken with a sharp tongue. Beatrice didn't feel like capping off her fairly relaxing day by a dark mountain drive with a poor driver and a cranky passenger.

"Thanks, but I'll drive myself," said Beatrice hurriedly.

Meadow frowned. "You want to pick *me* up, then?"

"To be honest, Meadow, I don't know how long I want to stay at Arabella's party. I wouldn't want to drag you out of there before you're ready. It's better if I just meet you there."

Meadow shrugged. "Okey-doke. See you later, then."

With that, Meadow made her farewell and hurried out the door.

Wyatt chuckled as he locked the door behind her. "Something like being caught in a hurricane, isn't it?"

"Something like that," said Beatrice with a sigh. "We were having such a nice, quiet time together, too. During your busy season."

Wyatt's eyes crinkled. "I think Christmas qualifies as most people's busy season. We can pick right up where we left off, you know. Hot chocolate, Christmas music, the fire, the corgi."

Noo-noo tilted her head to one side, smiling.

"Honestly, it's pitiful, but that brief visit absolutely wore me out. I might need to have a nap so I'll make it to the party later."

Wyatt said, "That's probably a good idea. Are you sure you can't skip it, though? Call the hostess and give a late RSVP?"

Beatrice shook her head. "I probably need to go. I promised Posy that I'd make it there. Meadow will be there, of course, but you know how Meadow is at a party. She's like a bee flying from one flower to another. Posy can be a little shy at parties and would like me there at first, at least."

"You're a good friend," said Wyatt, meaning it.

"Sometimes," said Beatrice. "Although I could probably handle Meadow a little better than I do. I was thinking while she was here that I should make a New Year resolution to work on my patience."

It turned out Noo-noo was just as delighted to accompany Beatrice to her nap as she had been at the idea of more quiet time by the fireplace. She snuggled up to Beatrice's side and was quickly making little doggy snores. Beatrice found herself drifting off to sleep.

It seemed like just a couple of minutes later when Wyatt gently shook her awake. "I can't remember exactly when the party starts, but I'm guessing you might need to wake up."

Noo-noo blearily sat up in bed as Beatrice jolted awake. "Heavens," she groaned, looking at her watch. "I should have been there fifteen minutes ago." She fumbled for her phone and typed out a text for Posy. Then she swung her legs off the bed and headed over to the closet. Fortunately, she'd already planned what she was wearing, so she could just pull on the black slacks and the festive red blouse. She dressed them up a little with a gold locket and earrings.

"You look great," said Wyatt when she walked out of the bedroom a few minutes later. "I can't even tell that you just woke up."

"Thanks," said Beatrice ruefully. "I had to splash my face and put on more makeup than I usually do. And thanks for waking me up."

"I really hated doing it because you were sleeping so soundly. But I knew you wanted to go to the party."

As Beatrice drove over, she reflected that *wanting* to go to the party was really the wrong word. She felt more *obligated* to go to the party. Although she had to admit that she had the feeling the party would prove interesting. Arabella Chamberlain was giving it at her home, which was a mansion on the top of a mountain. Although Arabella had grown up in Dappled Hills, she'd moved away decades earlier, only moving into her new home a few months ago. Beatrice had never been inside, but was interested in finding out what it looked like in there. She'd heard that the catering was supposed to be excellent and had the feeling there'd be plenty of good food to be had. Plus, some of her friends from the quilt guild were going to be there, which would also make it fun.

Having jollied herself into a good mood for the party, she felt much peppier as she approached the mansion. It looked rather majestic perched on the snow-covered mountain. The home itself was a blend of Southern elegance and modern luxury, with stucco walls and huge arched windows that sparkled in the moonlight. There were topiaries dusted with snow and twinkling yellow lights outlining the roof and windows. There was a wide, circular driveway with an illuminated fountain at its center. A valet walked up to her, which made her sigh with relief because she had absolutely no idea where she should park.

Beatrice hurried through the front door and into a grand foyer with a sweeping staircase draped with garlands and red velvet ribbons. A large crystal chandelier hung from the high ceiling, the light reflecting off the marble floor. From what Beatrice could see, every room was decorated to the hilt with poinsettias, Christmas trees, and evergreen wreaths. She spotted Posy, who gave her a big grin and wave, in the living room, which featured a massive stone fireplace, a roaring fire, and plush sofas in clusters.

"Sorry I'm late," said Beatrice. "I took a nap that didn't want to stop."

Posy's eyes twinkled. "A 'long winter's nap,' just like the poem. That sounds lovely. And I've been just fine. I didn't think I'd know many people here, but quite a few of my customers have chatted with me."

Posy owned the Patchwork Cottage quilt shop in downtown Dappled Hills. The little mountain shop was a popular spot for crafty folks, and Posy hosted a good number of workshops there. Beatrice wasn't surprised that she knew people at Arabella's party.

Posy confided in a quiet voice, "I still sort of feel out of place here, though."

"Who wouldn't?" Beatrice thought of the cozy cottage she shared with Wyatt. The mansion was elegant and beautiful, but didn't seem like a warm and inviting space to her.

"Did Wyatt come with you?" asked Posy.

"No, he's staying back at the house tonight. You know how busy life is for ministers this time of year. And he'll have to be up early tomorrow for church."

Posy's eyes twinkled again. "You won't be up early to go with him?"

"Not this time. This time the minister's wife will be sleeping in. Considering how hard I slept during that nap, I'm guessing

I need to get a couple of extra hours. I have the feeling you do, too, right? I know your shop gets crazy near Christmas."

Posy nodded, looking happy. "It's been a blur, a wonderful blur. Naturally, I had some really organized quilters who decided on their Christmas projects early and started making them in July."

"I'm hoping you're going to say the vast majority waited until after Thanksgiving," said Beatrice with a grin. "That will make me feel better about my own quilting procrastination."

"Right! Yes, most of them realized Christmas was practically upon us sometime last month. They've been rushing in to get materials for wall hangings, stuffed animals, or clothing. And they're usually in a tizzy because they have to allow for shipping times for some things they're making, if they're gifts for family they're not seeing during the holiday. And this past week, I saw lots of husbands coming in getting gift cards for their wives."

There was a blur of color out of the corner of Beatrice's eye and suddenly Meadow was upon them, looking as if she was fresh as a daisy, despite her busy Saturday preparing for the craft show. She was wearing an eclectic collection of garments, a skirt, a top, a scarf, a belt, that were all in different colors, but seemed to work well on Meadow.

"Why are the two of you hiding out in here?" Meadow demanded.

Chapter Two

Posy and Beatrice looked at each other. Beatrice said, "I think we were just relaxing and catching up. It's nice to take a breather every now and then." The last might have been said a bit pointedly.

"But there's so much to do and see! You both have fireplaces at home. Come on, let's take a lap around the place. You're at a *party*."

Beatrice and Posy dutifully followed Meadow. The first stop was a lavish buffet of food, with caterers hovering nearby to make sure everything was refreshed as soon as they ran out. There was also another table set up close to the buffet. Beatrice looked at it curiously.

"It's a *caviar* bar. A caviar bar! Can you believe it?" asked Meadow.

Beatrice wasn't at all sure that she liked caviar, but she was very impressed. She had the feeling it was the first time that Dappled Hills had had anything like a caviar bar. In fact, she wasn't at all sure where Arabella would have sourced the food. It certainly didn't come from Bub's Grocery, which sold a limited amount of fairly pedestrian stock.

"There's also a sushi station," bubbled Meadow. "It has fresh sashimi, hand rolls, and all sorts of exotic sauces."

Posy and Beatrice looked at each other again. Beatrice hadn't had such exotic food since she'd moved away from Atlanta and retired from her art museum and the gala fundraisers it held. She had the feeling her tummy might go on strike unless she had something more familiar to eat.

Posy leaned closer to Meadow as if worried someone might overhear. "Do you think there's more basic food? What's in the buffet?"

Meadow led them back over to it and made a sweeping hand gesture. And suddenly, Beatrice found herself hungry. It looked as if it was simpler fare with a twist. There were sausage rolls in puff pastry, but with truffle-infused mustard. There was a little sign pointing out vol-au-vents, pastry shells filled with a mix of wild mushrooms, Greek yogurt, garnished with fresh herbs. There were also shepherd's pie and vegetable lasagna served in small, elegant portions.

Beatrice and Posy didn't need more persuading as they filled their plates with food. Meadow waited impatiently, practically hopping with energy. "I still haven't shown you all the other stuff."

Beatrice said in a reasonable tone, "Posy and I are going to refuel first. Unless we can see everything while eating at the same time."

Posy's brow furrowed. "You know, I haven't seen Miss Sissy. Didn't you say you were bringing her to the party, Meadow?"

Meadow grinned at her. "She's one of the things I need you two to see."

Beatrice's curiosity was finally piqued. She couldn't imagine what could tear Miss Sissy away from a bounteous buffet like this one. The old woman's appetite was unrelenting. Beatrice wasn't sure where all the food went, considering the fact she was likely a hundred pounds soaking wet.

They followed Meadow down a festively lit corridor lined with more Christmas trees. Each tree had its own theme. One looked straight out of a fairy tale, perhaps Hansel and Gretel minus the witch and oven. Or maybe from *Charlie and the Chocolate* Factory. It was covered with candy cane stripes, lollipop ornaments, gingerbread men, and multicolored gumdrops. The topper was a giant, swirling peppermint candy.

Another tree's theme was a peacock. Beatrice decided it should look quite odd and out of place since it wasn't Christmas themed, but it was unexpectedly spectacular. Covered with teal, emerald, and gold ornaments, it had peacock feathers gracefully interspersed among the branches. The lights were rich purple and blue, and it was topped by a stunning peacock plume arrangement, which was fanned out majestically.

Meadow was delivering a chatty monologue about everything around her. The feathers, the colors, the themes, the music playing from a couple of different areas. Then she asked Beatrice and Posy, "How's your food?"

"Delicious," Posy and Beatrice chorused, as if they'd rehearsed it.

"Have you two seen Arabella at all?" Beatrice asked Posy and Meadow.

They shook their heads. "I was on the sofa the whole time," admitted Posy.

Meadow said, "Well, I've been all around, but I haven't seen Arabella. I'm sure she's just flitting from one room to another, making sure everything is perfect. Which, of course, it is."

They finally reached another large room where carolers dressed in Victorian attire were singing *O, Holy Night*. The carolers appeared completely authentic with the men in frock coats, high-waisted trousers, and top hats. Beatrice had the feeling the poor women were corseted and hoop-skirted. Bonnets with ribbons framed their faces. The only odd thing was a discordant sound. A terrible, croaking, persistently discordant sound that seriously detracted from the carolers.

"Oh dear," said Posy.

It was indeed Miss Sissy. The remains of several plates of food perched precariously on the table next to her. The old woman had apparently also made at least two visits to the near-by champagne tower, judging from the empty glasses next to her. She was enthusiastically singing along. It was surprising, since Miss Sissy was usually so taciturn, sparing few words for anyone.

"It would be better if she weren't singing so loudly," pointed out Meadow helpfully.

"Do you think we should do something about it?" asked Posy, looking concerned. "Maybe we should just scoop her up and walk her back to the buffet."

Beatrice smiled. Miss Sissy looked so happy with her drink, her food, and her carols. "I don't think she's doing any harm. Aside from Miss Sissy, no one else is really listening to the carolers; they're just background music to people's conversations. And it doesn't look like they mind."

Indeed, the carolers were hiding smiles of their own, practically encouraging the old woman to join them. So Beatrice, Meadow, and Posy continued on their voyage of exploration around the tremendous house.

"There's also a hot chocolate bar farther down," offered Meadow. "That might be kind of fun."

Posy said, "I've never heard of a hot chocolate bar. What does it have?"

"Oh, different types of gourmet hot chocolate."

"There are different types of hot chocolate?" Posy sounded rather stunned to hear this.

"Sure, there are," said Meadow. "And none of them are the powdered stuff we can pick up at Bub's Grocery. The signs said 'classic hot chocolate,' 'decadent hot chocolate,' 'creamy white chocolate,' and 'spiced Mexican chocolate.' You can top it with whipped cream, crushed candy canes, chocolate shavings, toffee bits, caramel drizzle, and cinnamon sticks. Oh, and you can add espresso shots or Irish cream."

Beatrice had the feeling she would need to take Noo-noo on lots of brisk walks after this party. But she wasn't wanting to escape just yet. It was definitely an interesting experience. The kind of party where anything could happen.

To prove her point, Meadow said, "There are supposed to be fireworks soon. They should look really spectacular against the mountain backdrop."

Beatrice spotted a cluster of empty armchairs along a wide corridor where they could sit and watch people. "Why don't we have a seat here? Posy and I haven't finished our food yet."

Posy chuckled. "We've been too busy talking and gaping at everything to eat."

"And still no sign of Arabella," said Beatrice.

They sat in the plush armchairs upholstered in a rich, velvety fabric. A small, ornate table sat between the chairs, holding a vintage lamp. Luxurious throw pillows and blankets were draped over the armchairs.

Meadow chatted excitedly while Posy and Beatrice made good progress with their food. "There's never been a Christmas party like this in Dappled Hills. Never! Right, Posy?"

Posy was also a long-time resident and shook her head in agreement.

Meadow said, "Of course, not everybody in town is here to see it, but I did see a reporter from the paper and a photographer taking pictures. People will be amazed when they see the pictures in the newspaper."

"Are there many people here we know?" asked Beatrice, polishing off the food remaining on her plate.

"I've seen probably thirty people we know. June Bug is here, helping with the cakes. We haven't even come across the pastries and cakes yet," said Meadow, a bit pointedly.

June Bug was another member of the Village Quilters. She was both an excellent quilter, and an accomplished baker. She owned a bakery in downtown Dappled Hills.

"Did June Bug make all the desserts for the party?" Beatrice frowned. "That would be a tremendous job. There must be over a hundred people here."

"No, there's some bigwig pastry chef who's doing a lot of it. But Arabella apparently wanted to 'shop local' and hire June Bug," said Meadow.

Beatrice said, "That's hardly a sacrifice, considering how good June Bug's cakes are."

Posy's eyes widened. "Isn't that Arabella now?"

They looked over at a beautiful woman in her mid-40s, wearing an emerald dress and stiletto heels. Her dark hair was pulled into an up-do. Meadow called out to her, but she didn't hear and continued setting off with determination toward the back of the house.

"I wonder if she's making sure the fireworks are ready to go," said Posy.

Meadow snorted. "At a party like this? I bet she has a party planner in charge of all that stuff."

Beatrice frowned. "Doesn't Arabella have something to do with parties? Or events? She owns her own business, doesn't she?"

"If she does, it can't be based here. We don't even have reliable internet some days," pointed out Meadow.

Posy squinted as if trying to dredge the information about Arabella's occupation out of her brain. "It's got to be something that does really, really well. Maybe she's a day trader?"

"Or a hedge fund manager," suggested Meadow.

Posy's eyes opened wide. "You don't think she's a drug dealer? Or doing something else illegal?"

Beatrice grinned at them. "I think your imaginations are running away with you. It's probably something totally prosaic. Maybe she inherited the money." She pulled out her phone from her purse. "I just happen to have a miniature computer right here that can tell me what she does."

Meadow looked delighted. "The internet! Why don't I ever think about the internet?"

Beatrice did a quick search for Arabella Chamberlain. "Okay, it looks like she owns an event planning and design company."

Meadow raised her eyebrows. "If this party is an example of what she can do, no wonder she's making money."

Beatrice scrolled on her phone. "The business covers everything from upscale weddings to galas, to large corporate events."

"Weddings? I can't even imagine having a huge wedding like this party," said Posy. "Cork and I had our wedding and reception in the courtyard of the church. There weren't more than twenty people there. I wore just a basic tea-length dress with a veil I made."

Beatrice nodded. "Exactly. But some people apparently go all the way with them." She looked down at her phone again. "Arabella's company turns barns and other outdoor spaces into these amazing venues. The wedding gowns are all bespoke. And the receptions look out of this world."

Meadow spread out her hands in supplication. "So how did we end up on the guest list? I mean, seriously."

Beatrice said wryly, "I hate to say it, but I have the feeling it has more to do with who our husbands are than who we are."

Meadow said, "Ah! I think you've hit on it, Beatrice. So I'm married to the chief of police of Dappled Hills."

Beatrice said, "And technically, Arabella is a member of Wyatt's congregation, although I haven't seen her there but once."

Posy's brow furrowed. "I'm a little confused about why Cork would have gotten an invite." Cork owned the wine store downtown.

Beatrice said, "Okay, I think you're the only one who was probably invited on her own recognizance. Or at least equally with your husband. You're both business owners." She glanced around her. "Most of the folks I've seen here have probably flown into Asheville, rented a car, and driven here to Dappled Hills. They've got to be business acquaintances of Arabella's."

Posy pushed her glasses up her nose. "Have either of you met Arabella?"

Beatrice said, "Just once, after a church service. She introduced herself to Wyatt and me."

Meadow said, "I haven't actually met her at all. I tried my best to catch up with her at the grocery store one time, but she was charging around so fast that I couldn't."

Posy nodded. "I haven't met her, either. That's one reason I felt a little funny attending the party tonight."

"Well, we'll make sure we speak to her," said Beatrice with determination. She felt there was no way she could leave the party without at least thanking the hostess.

"Is Arabella married?" asked Meadow. "Did the internet say anything about that?"

Beatrice said, "Her social media didn't mention a husband, and it looked like she stayed on top of updating that. So I'm going to say no."

Posy said, "I should find a glass of water." She glanced behind them and chuckled. "I'm just not sure I *can* find a drink of water."

"Yeah, the servers seem to be circulating wine," said Beatrice dryly.

Meadow stood up. "I can find water for us. I could probably use some, too."

"I'll go with you," said Posy. "Want some, Beatrice?"

"Sounds good. I'll save our chairs for us."

As they set off, Beatrice settled back into the plush armchair. She could hear the carolers in the distance, the buzz of conversation spiked with laughter from the guests, and, just faintly, a closer conversation, one taking place just a few yards away.

"I mean, she knows how to throw a good party, but Arabella is really just an awful human being." It was a woman's voice, sounding peevish.

Another woman said, "Aren't you exaggerating a little? So she was short with the party staff. Arabella's under a lot of stress right now, after all?"

"Because of a party?" scoffed the first woman. "That's no excuse to treat people who work for you like that. And that pastry chef she was talking to is supposed to be the top of her field. Arabella spoke to her like she was an idiot."

The women were quiet for a few moments. Then the second woman said, "Look over there. That's Ruth, Arabella's sister. They're nothing at all alike, are they?"

"No. Ruth has always been so plain and inconspicuous. It's hard to believe she's related to Arabella."

The second woman said, "Right? Arabella is gorgeous, even if she is a pain."

The conversation switched to food, and the two set off to investigate the options. That's when Posy and Meadow returned with three waters. Meadow said, "Boy, finding water wasn't as easy as you'd think. You could get any kind of mixed drink or frozen cocktail, but the servers totally froze when you asked where water was."

"Thanks for finding it," said Beatrice. She took a big sip, then another. Maybe it was the warmth of the room, especially with all the guests, that was making her thirsty.

There was a cracking sound outside, and then a bright plume of light lit up the outdoors.

"The fireworks!" said Meadow, standing up. "Come on, let's head out there."

"What about our plates?" asked Posy, not wanting to sully the mansion in any way. But as if he were telepathic, a member of the event staff, dressed in a crisp black-and-white uniform, glided toward them in a move that almost appeared choreographed. He smiled at them and quickly took away Posy and Beatrice's plates before disappearing again.

Meadow watched him leave. "Wouldn't it be nice to have someone like him at home? He could tail Ramsay as he left his path of destruction around the house. We'd keep everything clean as a whistle with someone like him around." She gestured to Beatrice and Posy impatiently. "Come on! Let's see the fireworks."

They stepped out of double doors that led to a tremendous terrace overlooking the mountains, visible in the moonlight. The terrace had wrought-iron railings, potted plants of all sorts, and expensive-looking outdoor furniture. It also provided an unobstructed view.

A firework exploded into the darkness, with silver and blue accents that twisted into a pattern before fading away.

"A snowflake!" the women chorused.

The snowflake was soon followed in rapid succession with a Star of Bethlehem, silver bells, and candy cane swirls. The atmosphere on the terrace was very convivial, thought Beatrice. The sophisticated strangers felt like part of their group as they oohed and ahhed together.

Afterwards, they quickly walked back in. They'd been so distracted by the beautiful fireworks that they hadn't felt the December chill. As soon as they were over, though, they were ready to head back inside and warm up at one of the roaring fires that the staff were keeping stoked.

Meadow was about to continue dragging them around the mansion when they saw June Bug, a small woman with a round face and a constantly startled expression running up to them in a panic.

June Bug's face was deathly pale, and Beatrice caught hold of her. "What's wrong, June Bug?" she asked.

"Is Ramsay here?" she asked Meadow breathlessly.

"No, he's back at the house. What is it?" Meadow was already pulling out her phone to call her husband.

"It's Nadia," said June Bug, gasping. "The pastry chef. She's dead."

Chapter Three

Beatrice recalled later how the party, unwittingly, continued, perhaps sounding more raucous than it had when she'd arrived as the amount of alcohol consumed grew. Meadow and Posy stood guard at the front of the hallway that led to the huge kitchen to prevent partygoers from accidentally wandering down there. Ramsay, the police chief, was on his way. Beatrice, careful not to touch anything, walked into the kitchen to confirm Nadia was indeed past needing medical help.

Nadia was a woman who looked to be in her thirties with dark locks pulled back from her face in a ponytail. She wore classic chef's whites, pristine and starched aside from the blood spatters from the rolling pin that killed her. Nadia's body was a stark, frightening sight in the massive kitchen with its mahogany cabinetry, polished marble floors, and commercial-grade range.

Beatrice wrapped her arms around herself, feeling cold once more. There was no question Nadia was dead. She turned and walked back to join the others at the front of the hall.

As Beatrice walked up, a young man in his twenties with dark hair was waving his hands around as he talked to Meadow.

June Bug was leaning against the wall, a shocked look on her round face. When she spotted Beatrice, she hurried over. "She's dead?"

"I'm afraid so."

June Bug's face fell. "I was hoping I was wrong."

Meadow said, "Ramsay's going to be here in just a moment." She gave June Bug a concerned look.

Beatrice turned to the young man. He appeared to be part of the event staff, judging from his black-and-white uniform. He noticed her glancing at him and said, "I'm Liam Quinn. I was assisting Nadia with the pastries."

"You're a pastry chef?" asked Beatrice.

He cleared his throat. "An apprentice, yes. I'm in an apprenticeship with Nadia." Beatrice found his expression unreadable.

June Bug wiped a stray tear from her cheek. "Liam was with me when I found Nadia."

Before Beatrice or anyone else could ask more questions, Ramsay suddenly joined them. He was a short, balding man who'd enjoyed many years of Meadow's Southern cooking. He was short of breath from his hurry to join them. "She's in there?" he asked, gesturing with his head toward the end of the hall.

Meadow nodded. "We kept everyone away."

Ramsay strode off, returning after a couple of minutes with a grim expression on his face. "Okay," he said. "Meadow, I need you to track down the hostess and tell her that everybody needs to stay here until the police can talk to them. I saw some sound systems in the house, so have her make an announcement." He turned to Posy, who looked sweetly earnest, ready to take on an assignment. "Posy, could you continue to make sure no one comes down this hall?"

Posy nodded, and for a second, Beatrice thought she might be about to salute.

Ramsay asked, "Beatrice, who discovered the pastry chef?"

Beatrice looked over at the miserable-looking June Bug. "June Bug did, but she wasn't alone. The apprentice pastry chef was with her." She glanced around. "He was just here, but it looks like he's walked off."

Ramsay said, "Can you find him and bring him over to me while I make a phone call to the state police? And June Bug, if you could just stay here for a few minutes so I can talk with you after I make my phone call?"

Beatrice hurried off to find the young man. Liam, she thought he'd said his name was. It seemed very wrong that the party was so enthusiastically continuing when a woman had lost her life in the kitchen. She hoped Meadow could find Arabella soon. But then, Arabella had been rather elusive the entire evening. It had reminded her of *The Great Gatsby,* where the host of the lavish parties was nowhere to be found.

Beatrice decided that a young man, clearly relieved of his pastry duties by the tragedy, might want to head over to the food or the alcohol first. Sure enough, she found him over by a long table full of different wines. "Liam," she called to him, hoping that was indeed his name.

He turned around, giving her a quizzical look.

"The police want to talk with you. Can you come back to the kitchen with me?"

Liam frowned. "The police? But I had nothing to do with what happened. They're not going to get any information from me."

"I think it's standard procedure, since you found Nadia."

A woman who was pouring herself a drink turned to stare, a frown punctuating her brow.

"Just come with me," said Beatrice impatiently.

Liam came along, carrying his wineglass. "It was a shock," he muttered to excuse the beverage.

They wove their way through the throngs of partygoers to the kitchen. Ramsay had finished his phone call and was speaking with June Bug. June Bug looked relieved as Beatrice approached.

"Liam?" asked Ramsay. "You're the one who found the pastry chef, correct?"

"Well, with this lady, here," said Liam, gesturing to June Bug. "Arabella was in a tizzy because some pastries hadn't come out yet. So we walked to the kitchen to grab them or ask Nadia where they were. And when we walked into the kitchen, we saw her." Liam shrugged.

"Is that what happened?" Ramsay's voice was gentler when he spoke to June Bug. She quickly nodded, lifting her hand to swipe away a stray tear.

"When was the last time you saw the pastry chef? Nadia, her name was?"

June Bug looked like she was trying to reach back into her memory and pull that particular moment out. While she was thinking, Liam inserted himself. "Nadia Danvers was her name. I was with Nadia most of the time the last couple of days."

"And tonight?" asked Ramsay.

Liam shrugged again. "I was with her most of the time again. I was her apprentice, so my job was to shadow her, be her gofer, help her out in the kitchen, that kind of thing."

Ramsay nodded. "So, if you were shadowing her, you must have been close by when this happened. Correct?"

"Yeah, but Nadia was also having me run over to the serving tables to see what the guests were running out of. Then I'd grab them from the kitchen and put them out. I wasn't *always* in the kitchen."

Ramsay turned to look thoughtfully at June Bug, who looked startled. He said kindly, "And you? I know you were supplying cakes for the party, but why were you in the kitchen?"

June Bug swallowed. "I was . . . learning. Nadia is very, very famous."

Ramsay frowned. "Is she?"

Liam snorted. "Famous in baking circles. She was not exactly a celebrity in any other way."

"Okay," said Ramsay calmly. "So June Bug, you were learning from Nadia, sort of like Liam here?"

Beatrice wouldn't have thought June Bug needed to learn anything at all. Everything she'd ever eaten over at the bakery had been exquisite. The only reason she didn't visit the bakery every day is because she'd be as big as the side of the barn Meadow lived in if she did.

June Bug nodded eagerly. "Yes! I wanted to learn more. Nadia makes really *artistic* desserts. I asked her if I could shadow her today."

Ramsay looked back at Liam. "So you left the kitchen."

"Headed to the restroom," said Liam curtly.

"Okay. And June Bug? Why did you leave the kitchen?"

June Bug said, "I was going to say hi to my friends for a minute."

Ramsay nodded. "And then Arabella approached both of you?" He tilted his head to one side. If Liam were in the restroom and June Bug was looking for her friends, they'd hardly be in the same location.

Liam quickly said, "I stepped out to see the fireworks for a minute. When Arabella spotted us and waved us over, we were close by. She told us to get the pastries out and we headed to the kitchen to grab them."

"Did you talk to anyone along the way to the kitchen? Did either of you see anything out of place or unusual?"

Liam and June Bug looked at each other. Liam said, "No, I don't remember seeing anything out of the ordinary."

June Bug cleared her throat. She said in almost an apologetic voice, "There was that woman? The crying woman."

Chapter Four

L iam snapped his fingers. "Right."

"The crying woman?" asked Ramsay.

June Bug said, "There was this blonde lady who was crying near the kitchen."

Ramsay's eyes were intent. "How near the kitchen? Had she been in there?"

Liam interrupted. "Maybe. She was really upset about something. Maybe she argued with Nadia about something, killed her, then felt sorry about it."

Beatrice had the feeling Liam was grasping at straws, trying to find somebody who'd take the fall for Nadia's death.

"What did this woman look like?" Ramsay glanced at both June Bug and Liam.

June Bug repeated, "Blonde." Then she gave a helpless shrug to show that was all she had.

Liam was either more observant or more determined to find a scapegoat for the murder. "She was short, kind of plump. Her hair was thick. She was angry-crying, come to think of it, so maybe she wasn't sorry at all about killing Nadia."

Ramsay gave him a wry look. Liam was clearly trying to blame the crying woman for everything. "Are you sure she just didn't have too much to drink? There's been a lot of drinking going on here, as far as I can tell."

Liam said, "It's a party. Yeah, there's been drinking. But she was the only person crying. I didn't really get the impression she was drunk."

Ramsay focused again on Liam. "Going back to Nadia. How did this apprenticeship come about?"

Liam quirked a dark brow. "You're really interested in this? From what I saw, there's a murder that's probably a little more pressing."

Ramsay said in a deceptively laid-back voice, "Let's just say that I'd like to know how the whole set-up works. I understand June Bug's shadowing stuff, but I don't understand what this program of yours looks like."

Liam blew out a breath. "Okay. I'm going to community college to get an Associate in Applied Science, Culinary Arts." A brief look of pride crossed his features. "I'm specializing in baking and pastry arts. Part of our curriculum is to get internships or externships with chefs. Sometimes the school helps do the matchmaking and sometimes organizations like the American Culinary Federation will match students up with experienced chefs."

"And they picked Nadia for you?" asked Ramsay

"Well, I indicated that I'd like them to match me with Nadia. She's the top of her field, especially with advanced decoration. The idea is that she was to be a mentor, share her knowledge, and help me develop my own style."

"And did that happen?" asked Ramsay. "What was it like working with Nadia?"

June Bug seemed very intent on hearing the answer to that question. Beatrice wondered if maybe she had her own ideas about what it might have been like.

Liam said, "Yeah, she did all those things. But I still wasn't going to give her an amazing score when the school asked for us to rate our experience."

"Why is that?"

Liam said, "Because she's a perfectionist. And perfectionists are impossible to get along with. Know why? Because perfection is something that just can't be achieved by the perfectionist. They're always going to find something to pick apart, even if no one else can see it."

Ramsay asked, "So the two of you didn't get along?"

"Oh, I made *sure* we got along." Liam bared his teeth in a smile. "I knew what side my bread was buttered on. Look, I really needed an excellent recommendation from Nadia Danvers. Getting one would ensure I got into the finer restaurants as a pastry chef."

Ramsay nodded. "What did you think of Nadia?"

"Personally, or professionally?"

"Both," said Ramsay.

"Well, I thought she wasn't quite as wonderful as she thought she was. Don't get me wrong—there's a reason she's a celebrated pastry chef. But she wasn't just meticulous, she took it to another level. She sucked the joy out of the entire creative process. The whole reason most of us got into pastries is because we love the act of creating. We love sweets, too. I don't think Nadia even *liked* sweets. When she had to sample her pastries, she made a face like she was taking a spoonful of some awful medicine or something."

Ramsay took a few notes on the notepad he'd been writing on. "And her instruction? You said she did all right with showing you the ropes?"

"She did the bare minimum. But there were issues. I sometimes wondered if she *would* give me a good recommendation, even though I was kissing up to her. She was dismissive of any ideas that weren't hers. And she was harsh when anybody made mistakes, or what she thought were mistakes."

Ramsay nodded again. "So you kind of followed Nadia around on the different gigs she had, right? Obviously the two of you weren't stationed here."

"That's right. We were based in Virginia, but we traveled to wherever the event was."

Ramsay asked, "Did you get the impression she had friends? Anybody she was close to?"

Liam shook his head. "Nope. I think her drive for success totally derailed that. I don't know of any close personal relationships that she had."

Ramsay jotted down a couple more notes. "Did Nadia talk at all about her personal life?"

"Never. Nadia was always guarded. She didn't ever let on what was going through her mind. She kept her private life just that—private. Nobody really knew her outside of the kitchen."

Ramsay asked, "Can you think of anybody who might have been upset with Nadia? Anyone she's had issues with lately?"

Liam said, "Well, the housekeeper seemed like she was in a bad mood with Nadia today. But Nadia is so blunt that she probably said something to make her mad. Whether she'd have killed Nadia over whatever it was is debatable."

The state police came in just then with a forensics team. Ramsay said, "Okay. June Bug, I know where to find you if I have any further questions. Liam, if you could give me your contact information, I'd appreciate it."

Liam said, "Yeah, well, I'm going to be heading out of here, you know. This gig is over. I'll have to let my school know what happened to my apprenticeship and get in with somebody else."

Ramsay said, "I'd like you to stay in Dappled Hills for the next few days while we're investigating. You worked closely with Nadia, and I'm sure we'll have more questions for you."

Liam's eyes flashed. "I didn't kill Nadia, man. And I need to get back to school."

Ramsay didn't seem flustered by Liam's irritation whatsoever. "I'm sure your school will understand. Besides, it's December 16. I'm assuming you're about to start your Christmas break any day now."

Liam's sullen silence seemed to confirm this.

Ramsay headed off to talk to the state police. Liam quickly hurried off and out of sight. June Bug gave Beatrice a weak smile, and Beatrice hugged her.

"How are you doing?" asked Beatrice. "Are you holding up? Do you need a ride home?"

June Bug shook her head. "It's okay." She tried to make her smile bigger while wiping another stray tear.

They walked out toward Meadow and Posy. Meadow drew June Bug into a fierce hug. "So awful! I'm so sorry, June Bug. Can I drive you home?"

June Bug carefully shook her head. "No, thank you. Beatrice already offered. I'll be careful on the way back, but I need to get my car back home so I can make it to the bakery tomorrow. And I need to go now."

It was possibly the longest speech Beatrice had ever heard June Bug make.

Meadow's eyes widened. "Katy! Is she at the house by herself?"

Katy was June Bug's niece. She'd taken her in when her sister had died some time ago.

"Rowena is with her. But I need to let Rowena get back home, too." June Bug looked completely exhausted. Beatrice was sure that Katy wasn't the only one who needed to head to bed.

Meadow suddenly said, "Gracious, I need to collect Miss Sissy."

"She's not going to want to leave," said Posy, eyes twinkling. "She was having such a good time eating and singing."

Meadow strode off in the direction they'd last seen Miss Sissy. June Bug started toward the door, then stopped, staring at a nearby woman. She turned to look at Beatrice, her wide eyes even wider than usual.

Beatrice sidled closer. "You recognize that woman?"

June Bug gave her an earnest nod. "The crying woman." Then she hurried away, waving with one hand.

Beatrice looked closer at the woman, who was distracted by the police interviewing some guests a few yards away. She definitely recognized her. In fact, she was nearly certain that the woman was a member of their congregation. She'd have to look at the church's most recent directory to make sure. While the woman was looking in another direction, she took a surreptitious picture with her phone.

"Poor June Bug," said Posy sympathetically, looking after her as she scurried away. "What an awful thing to happen."

Meadow returned with Miss Sissy in tow. As expected, she was not amused to have been taken away from the party. Wiry gray hair had fallen out of her bun and was sticking out around her head. Although Meadow was cheerfully talking to her, the old woman appeared to be snarling at her.

Meadow said, "We should head out. Everyone else has to stick around, of course, until Ramsay and the other cops get their statements."

"Did Arabella make the announcement for all the guests to stay?" asked Beatrice.

"Somebody did," said Meadow, shrugging. "Some underling or other. At any rate, no one has left. Or, at least, conspicuously left. And the police are keeping everyone here now."

"How will *we* be able to leave then?" asked Posy, looking worried.

One side of Meadow's lip curled up in a smile. "Easy-peasy, when you're the wife of the police chief. I'll tell Ramsay that he'll need to talk with Miss Sissy later, if he needs to interview her. Although I think it's doubtful she knows anything vital."

Now Miss Sissy's snarl was even more pronounced.

Their group walked right out the door and the valets, who hadn't had anything else to do, brought their cars straight to them.

Beatrice did her best to put the night's events out of her mind as she slowly drove in the dark down the curvy mountain road. The last thing she needed was a distraction, especially considering the fact that the fog was creeping down. She breathed a sigh of relief when she pulled into her driveway and saw Noonoo's little furry face peeping at her from the window.

Wyatt had been asleep in front of the fire. He sat up when he heard Beatrice come inside. Rubbing his eyes, he said, "How was it? Is everything okay?"

Beatrice sank down next to him on the sofa. Noo-noo snuggled up to her, lying halfway across her legs. "I'm fine. But there was a murder at the party. Arabella's pastry chef was killed with a rolling pin in the kitchen."

"What?" Wyatt was now completely awake. Noo-noo nuzzled Beatrice with her nose, as if sensing her tension.

"June Bug and an apprentice chef found her." Beatrice shook her head. "Meadow called Ramsay, and he came right over. The state police had arrived by the time we left."

Wyatt frowned. "Was the pastry chef someone who works for June Bug?"

"No, she wasn't local. Her name was Nadia, and she was apparently a very celebrated chef." Beatrice shook her head. "It's such a crazy thing to murder someone at a big party like that. Anyone could have walked in on the killer. The house was massive, and it would have been easy for someone to have lost their way and wander back there."

"Was June Bug all right?" asked Wyatt. "She's such a gentle soul."

"She really is. She was crying, but rallied toward the end. She wanted to drive herself home, so she seemed okay."

Wyatt said slowly, "Is the murderer on the loose?"

Beatrice nodded, rubbing Noo-noo gently. "Yes. Ramsay spoke to the apprentice who worked with Nadia. It sounded like she might not have been the most popular person to be around. A big perfectionist. She might have been sort of curt with people. It's hard to believe somebody would murder her over that, though."

Wyatt reached out a hand to her, and they sat quietly, watching the fire die out.

Chapter Five

The next morning, Beatrice woke earlier than expected. Wyatt was already ready for church and eating breakfast. He looked at her in surprise as she walked out of the bedroom.

"Sorry, did I wake you up? You were going to sleep in this morning."

Beatrice said ruefully, "You had nothing to do with it. My sleep schedule is all messed up. I think I'll go to church after all this morning. Maybe it'll help me feel more settled after the craziness of last night."

"Should I wait so we can go together?"

Beatrice said, "No, you go on ahead. It's going to take me some time to get myself looking decent enough to go. I may have to make myself another pot of coffee to really wake up, too."

Wyatt headed out a few minutes later while Beatrice slowly went through the motions of getting ready for church. She was pleased to find her red, Christmassy blouse clean and hanging up. She hadn't remembered if she'd laundered it after church a couple of weeks ago, or if it was still lounging in the hamper, waiting to be washed.

She let Noo-noo out one more time, then headed out herself. Beatrice usually walked the short distance, but the snow that had fallen the night before was slushy and she didn't fancy getting her dress shoes muddy. As she got out of the car, she admired the church, its mossy gray stones covered with a dusting of snow.

A wind whipped up and Beatrice walked quickly inside. She was a bit later than she'd intended on being, and the organ prelude was already playing. She slipped into an empty spot in one of the wooden pews. As she'd hoped, she felt some of her stress drop from her as she sat quietly in the sanctuary. The Chrismon tree at the front was adorned with white and gold ornaments of Christian symbols. Poinsettias lined the steps to the pulpit and the advent wreath holding its candles of purple, pink, and white. Candles in glass lanterns perched on the windowsills, their flames dancing gently in front of the stained-glass windows.

Beatrice relaxed more as the service started and the familiar order of worship ran its course with hymns, readings, a church family lighting the next advent wreath candle, and the choir raising its collective voice in song. Wyatt gave a thoughtful sermon on the strength of Mary through uncertain times.

During the closing hymn, Beatrice glanced behind her to gauge how quickly she might make it out of the church and to the parking lot. Although she'd enjoyed the service, she didn't have any desire to stand with Wyatt and greet the departing congregation. Most days, it was a lovely way to end the service, but today she just wanted to head home and start making a hot lunch.

When she looked behind her, though, she was startled to see "the crying woman," as June Bug had called her. Beatrice had forgotten to look in the member directory or to show Wyatt the photo she'd taken before leaving Arabella's party the night before.

Now that she saw the woman again, she had an inkling of what her name might be. Melissa, she thought. She looked only marginally better than last night. Beatrice's quick glance had shown her Melissa's bloodshot eyes and the way she was almost shrinking down into her pew. Her thick blonde hair was pulled back in a neat bun.

Now Beatrice was thinking less about how quickly she could bolt from the church and how she might have a conversation with Melissa. She didn't want to scare the poor woman off, though. Beatrice had sensed how exhausted she seemed.

As soon as Wyatt gave the benediction and the choir finished the closing hymn, Beatrice stood up. Better to step outside, she decided. She could even head toward the parking lot and away from the large number of worshipers who'd gathered.

Before she could get too close to the parking lot, though, a soft voice called out to her. "Beatrice? It's Beatrice, isn't it?"

To her surprise, Beatrice found Melissa hurrying to catch up with her. She gave the smaller woman a warm smile. "Yes. You're Melissa?"

Melissa looked a little anxious. "You're the minister's wife, aren't you?"

"Yes, that's right." Beatrice paused. Out in the pale sunlight, Melissa looked even more exhausted. "Are you all right?"

Melissa gave a short laugh. "All right? Not particularly." She looked behind them with impatience as families started heading in their direction. "Can we go somewhere where we can talk privately? Maybe grab a coffee?"

Beatrice said, "Let's go to my house. I'm not sure a coffeehouse is all that private, and we live right next door. Are you okay with dogs?"

"I love them."

So Melissa followed Beatrice in her car. When they pulled into the driveway, Noo-noo's ears, then grinning face showed in the picture window at the front of the house. It was almost as if the little dog sensed a mission and was ready to take it on. The stone cottage looked welcoming, with a big wreath on the front door. Beatrice unlocked the door and greeted Noo-noo with a few pets, then invited Melissa inside.

As they walked in, Beatrice saw her home through Melissa's eyes. The hardwood floors creaked in protest as they trod on them. Beatrice gestured to an overstuffed gingham armchair, its slightly worn cushions a testament to years of being one of the best seats in the house. The walls were adorned with Southern folk art from Beatrice's days of museum curator, as well as corn husk dolls dressed in holiday attire. The surfaces were cluttered with family photos, Will's preschool artwork, and a couple of dying houseplants. The Frasier fir Christmas tree was loaded with ornaments, from a log cabin patterned fabric ornament to hand-carved wooden stars a member had made for Wyatt, and a gourd ornament featuring a winter scene. In addition, there was an old and well-loved nativity, a collection of Nutcrackers on top of the mantel, and a few jolly folk art Santas nestled around the room.

"I'll be right back with the coffee," said Beatrice in a cheery voice as she strode to the kitchen. She sent Wyatt a quick text as a heads-up. A few minutes later, she put the coffee carafe, sugar, and cream on a small table in front of Melissa. They fixed their coffee and then Beatrice settled across from Melissa on the edge of the sofa.

"Your dog and I have been getting acquainted," said Melissa with a weary smile. Noo-noo lay on Melissa's feet. "She's very sweet. And I love your house."

"Sorry about the mess," said Beatrice automatically.

"No, it's very tidy, but it looks *lived* in. I can't stand going to houses that look like showcases." Melissa frowned.

"Well, no worries about that here," said Beatrice lightly. She paused. "Although you might have thought that about Arabella's house last night. I believe I saw you there."

Melissa leaned forward, setting her coffee on an end table. "That's why I wanted to talk to you. About the party." She took a deep breath. "I found out my husband is cheating on me. Or *was* cheating on me. I went to the party last night to confront the woman he was having the fling with."

Beatrice kept quiet, waiting for Melissa to keep going. She wanted her to feel comfortable enough to tell her what was worrying her. Her concern was that Melissa was going to change her mind, make up some excuse, apologize, and leave.

Melissa took a deep breath. "I wasn't invited to the party or anything. Neither was my husband. He's out of town for work, actually, leaving me lots of time to stew over stuff."

Beatrice nodded, keeping quiet.

"The last week or so, my husband—his name is Hal—has been acting totally differently. He's been dreamy and distracted." She grimaced. "Lovesick, I guess, although I didn't realize it at the time. I was seriously thinking something was wrong with him, like maybe he had the flu or something. Then I noticed he kept putting away his phone and looking guilty when I came into the room. I finally managed to grab his phone and take a look when he was in the shower one day. I found out he was having an affair with that pastry chef who came into town to help Arabella with the party."

Beatrice held her breath. She hoped she wasn't about to get a murder confession. She'd have to persuade Melissa to go straight to Ramsay.

Melissa continued, "I kept mulling things over in my head. I told Hal I knew about the affair."

"What did he say?" asked Beatrice.

"He was furious with me for snooping on his phone. I mean, he was fuming. Isn't that crazy? He was acting like *I* was the one in the wrong. And he told me he wasn't having an affair at all, that it was just a fling."

Beatrice gave a sympathetic wince. Did it matter if it was a fling or an affair, or even a one-night-stand? The point was that he'd been unfaithful.

"So, Hal stomped off on his business trip while I made plans to crash Arabella's party and confront Nadia. I wanted to ask her who she thought she was to wreck my life in such a casual way, you know? I wanted her to be sorry. Because I can't take Hal back after this. I've thought about it, you know. I thought about talking with Wyatt about it, or even going into marriage counseling. I know other people have tried that and they're able to get their marriage back. But now I can't trust him. There's no way I can live with someone I can't trust. And Nadia took that from me."

Melissa gave her a rueful look. "I know that makes me sound vengeful and unforgiving."

Beatrice said, "Not at all. It makes you sound human. And like you've weighed this decision carefully."

"It was worse when Hal called me up, crying, yesterday. He apologized for snapping at me about snooping on his phone. He said he didn't know what had gotten into him—that he'd never cheated on me before. He said it would never happen again and begged me to take him back. But I stood my ground." Melissa sighed. "Hal seemed crushed. And after the call, I was stressed out, as you can imagine. It made me focus a lot of anger on Nadia. I wanted to give her a piece of my mind. And, of course, I didn't have a phone number for her, so I wanted to see her in person."

"What happened at the party?"

"Well, I figured she'd be in the kitchen, being a pastry chef and everything. That's where I headed." Melissa looked ruefully at Beatrice. "Don't worry. I did tell the cops all this, too. You don't have to worry about reporting me. Believe me, Ramsay is already all over my case. I obviously didn't have an alibi."

"Did you talk to Nadia? Or was she . . . already gone by the time you got to the kitchen?"

Melissa said, "Oh, she was still alive. It was a good time to go in there, because nobody else was in there. I guess they were all putting out more food. I'd practiced what I was going to say on the way over there, you know. I wanted to make Nadia feel as bad as possible in the short amount of time I had with her. When I got in there, though, my whole script flew out of my head."

"What was Nadia doing when you saw her?"

"Piddling around with some fancy pastry on the island. She barely even glanced up when I walked in. She just said in this sarcastic voice, 'You took a wrong turn. The party is that way. Don't drink so much next time.'"

"That must have been upsetting," said Beatrice. Upsetting wasn't quite the right word. Beatrice is sure she'd have been infuriated in Melissa's shoes. She was suddenly fervently grateful that Wyatt was such a good man and wonderful husband and didn't put her in those kinds of situations.

"Yeah. But I was so shocked that Nadia was talking to me that way that I couldn't seem to make words come out of my mouth. Not coherently, anyway. I was stuttering away, trying to make a connection between my brain and my mouth when she shot me this furious look and told me to get out of her kitchen."

Beatrice said slowly, "And you did?"

"I did. I just sort of shuffled out. Can you believe it? I burst into tears right after that. I couldn't understand how I could go so off-script. More than that, I didn't understand how I didn't have the self-respect to fire back at Nadia." Melissa gave a helpless shrug.

Beatrice said carefully, "I don't think you should feel bad about yourself at all. You were put in a difficult position, then you weren't expecting Nadia to be rude to you."

"No, I was expecting to be rude to *her*." Melissa gave a short laugh. She rubbed her eyes. "Sorry you've had to listen to all this. The whole reason I came over here was allegedly to find out what you knew about Nadia's death. The cops were keeping everything tight to their chests. I got the feeling they thought I was the prime suspect."

Beatrice shook her head. "They try to stay close-lipped about crime details, period, I think." She thought about how vague she could be. "All I know is that I was close by when some of the staff found Nadia. It sounded like it might have been a quick death." Surely death by rolling pin would have been speedy. At any rate, she hadn't been left alone for long, so she couldn't have suffered many minutes, if any. "I wish I had more information to give you."

Melissa gave her a crooked grin. "It's okay. I have the feeling that asking for information was more of an excuse, if I'm being honest. I've had all these thoughts about what happened last night whirling through my head. I needed to talk to somebody about them. Then, when I saw you at church, I thought you might be the best person to speak with."

"You know, Wyatt should be home any minute. You mentioned thinking about speaking with him about your marriage, but he might be helpful to sort out everything else on your mind. He's excellent at listening, and he has done a lot of counseling, too. You're always welcome to talk to me, but Wyatt might be more helpful."

Melissa flushed, shaking her head. "Wyatt was the one who married Hal and me. I'd feel embarrassed telling him that my marriage failed."

Beatrice reached across, impulsively grabbing her hand. "Don't think that way. Just know that we're here to listen, if you need us."

Melissa looked a little more cheerful at that. "That's true. Thanks, Beatrice. And thanks for being an ear. I really needed somebody to talk to."

With that, she took her coffee cup to the kitchen sink, gave Noo-noo one last rub, and headed out the door.

Chapter Six

Five minutes later, when Wyatt was walking in, Beatrice had finished her coffee.

"Everything good?" asked Wyatt cheerfully. "I spotted you near the back of the church."

"Great service," said Beatrice. "I wasn't much in the mood to socialize after all my socializing last night. But then I ended up getting a visitor after all."

"Really? Piper?"

Piper was Beatrice's daughter. She and her grandson, Will lived not too far away and often came by for a visit on a Sunday afternoon.

"No, Melissa Martin. Do you know her well?"

Wyatt said, "I wouldn't say I know her well, but I know who she is. She often comes over to greet me after the service, along with her husband Hal. Was there something special she needed?"

Beatrice considered what to say about Melissa's visit. She'd seemed reluctant to have Wyatt know about Hal's transgression. She decided to just stick with the bit that had to do with the party.

"Melissa was concerned because she's a suspect for Nadia's murder."

Wyatt sat down next to Beatrice, frowning. "Did she need me to call her?"

"I think she's okay now. She seemed to have a lot on her mind and wanted to tell someone about it." It was basically the truth.

There was a light tap at the front door.

"Gracious, we're popular," said Beatrice. But this was a very welcome visit. Piper came in wearing a cute Christmas sweater. Will toddled in, looking with interest at his rain boots.

"Snow!" he declared, pointing at the melting flakes on his boots.

"Yes, isn't the snow pretty? Did you play in it?" asked Beatrice.

Will nodded happily, plopping down on the floor so Piper could tug his boots off. He started wriggling away before she could take off his hat and mittens. Piper scooted in front of him to wrangle them off expertly.

Will ran over to Beatrice and gave one of her legs a hug.

"How's my big boy?" asked Beatrice.

"This big, Grandmama!" said Will proudly, holding his arms up as high as he could and nearly toppling over in the process.

Piper said, "Will, didn't you tell me you made something for Grandmama and Wyatt in Sunday school today?"

Will's small face lit up, and he ran over to his mom's purse. Rummaging inside, he pulled out a piece of paper with a Christmas tree drawn in the center by the teacher. Everywhere else on the piece of paper were red and green fingerprints.

"See?" he asked, looking up at Beatrice and smiling over at Wyatt.

"Wow!" said Wyatt, peering down at the paper. "It looks fantastic."

"Are these your fingerprints? You did an amazing job!" Beatrice said.

Will's face was proud. He held his little hands up, which still bore the evidence of the fingerpainting. "See?" he asked again.

"I can tell this is a very authentic piece," said Beatrice, nodding. "Want to find a spot on the fridge for it?"

Will ran off to rearrange magnets and put his artwork in a prime location on Beatrice and Wyatt's fridge. Beatrice decided it was a good thing that they had such an old fridge. Magnets wouldn't stick on the new stainless-steel fridges.

Beatrice looked wryly at Piper. "You and I together attended church for the full morning. You went to Sunday school, and I went to the service."

"You went to the service? I thought you were planning on sleeping in after the party last night."

Beatrice raised her eyebrows. "Nobody in Sunday school was talking about the party?"

"It was a small group today. I guess the people who went last night decided to stay in bed."

Will came running back over to join them. Wyatt quickly said to the boy, "How about if we play blocks?" He glanced over at Beatrice. "Then you can fill Piper in on what happened last night."

Beatrice said in a low voice, "Arabella's pastry chef was murdered at the party last night. June Bug found her."

"No! Was June Bug all right?"

"I think so, although I feel like I might want to check in on her today. I might head over to the bakery and just see."

Piper said, "Does she work on Sundays?"

"She bakes on Sundays, although the shop isn't open for customers. June Bug just works on open orders, cakes, and whatnot. Besides, I need to go downtown anyway to pick up the items for the angel tree." The angel tree provided gifts, warm clothing, toys, and other items for families who needed them at Christmas.

Piper said, "I can't believe someone would commit murder at a Christmas party. And with all those people around! Unless it wasn't as big a crowd as it sounded like it was going to be?"

"Oh, it was huge. There were tons of people in there. I'm guessing that it was completely unpremeditated. Somebody just got fed up with Nadia and lashed out."

Piper gave her a curious look. "What was the party like? Part of me was very interested in seeing the inside of the house."

"It was beautiful in there, but huge. Lots of Christmas trees, carolers, food, and drinks. It was like something out of a magazine spread. But it didn't look homey." Beatrice glanced around her small cottage, at the quilts, the throw rugs, the comfy furniture, her grandson's artwork, and the family photos. "I wouldn't trade my house for hers for all the money in the world."

"But it was fun to spend an evening there? I mean, aside from what happened."

"Sure it was. There was all this music and gourmet food and hot chocolate bars. I never got to speak to Arabella, the whole time I was there. It felt strange not to thank her for the party, but then the night ended so abruptly." Beatrice made a dismissive gesture. "Enough of what's going on in my world. Tell me about all the fun you, Ash, and Will are having."

Piper smiled. Her husband, Ash, was Meadow's son and a great husband and father. "Well, we decorated our tree a few days ago. Better late than never, I guess."

"It's still just December 17," said Beatrice kindly. "You have a lot going on between working at the school and being a mom. Don't sell yourself short. Will doesn't even know exactly when Christmas is."

"True," said Piper, brightening. "Will was absolutely thrilled to be helping put up the ornaments. I took a picture of the tree after we decorated it. I figured you might appreciate this."

Piper pulled up a photo on her phone and handed it to her mother. Beatrice took it and burst out laughing. The Christmas tree had clearly been decorated by a very short person. All the many ornaments were on the very bottom of the tree. In fact, each limb was weighed down by at least two, if not more, ornaments.

Piper gave Beatrice a rueful look. "Yeah. Ash and I thought about rearranging ornaments in other spots, but Will was so proud of his handiwork that we didn't have the heart."

"Like I said, this makes everything more authentic and homier. You'll have this picture and the story for the rest of your life. At Arabella's her trees were all decorated by theme."

"They must have been gorgeous," said Piper.

"They were. But you could tell that a designer had done them. It just didn't have the same feeling as your tree."

A grin tugged at the corner of Piper's mouth. "Our Charlie Brown Christmas tree?"

"It's a very sweet tree!"

Their conversation was interrupted by Will, who came hurrying away from the cityscape of blocks that he and Wyatt had built. "Hungwy? You hungwy?"

Beatrice thought it was a nice way for Will to approach the issue of getting fed. His ploy seemed to be to remind everyone that *they* were hungry. Then food would suddenly appear for everyone.

Beatrice said, "You know, Will, I think I *am* a little hungry. Let's have lunch."

Will looked relieved and grinned at her, showing off his baby teeth.

Piper said, "How about if I make everyone pancakes? Mama, why don't you put your feet up for a while?"

Beatrice leaned over to speak to Will. "How about a story?"

"Santa!" Will knew Beatrice had a collection of children's books in a coat closet. He also clearly remembered that she had Christmas books in there.

"I think I do have a Santa story in that closet," said Beatrice. "Why don't you go pull it out, since you're such a big boy?"

Will scampered off to the coat closet as Piper started putting together the pancake mix. Will returned just seconds later holding *The Night Before Christmas*, illustrated by Tasha Tudor. Will brandished the book at her excitedly. "Noo-noo!"

Tasha Tudor's books frequently included illustrations of corgis, and this book was no different. The sable-colored Pembroke on the cover with Santa looked very much like Noo-noo. Noo-noo, not sure why her name was being called, still seemed delighted at hearing it.

Will and Beatrice settled on the sofa with the corgi. Beatrice read the familiar poem while Will exclaimed over the different pictures. "Reindeer! Santa! Toys!" Wyatt set the table and got the syrup and butter out. By the time Will and Beatrice had finished reading, Piper was done with the pancakes.

Beatrice had remembered to pull out her everyday Christmas plates from the cabinet and run them through the dishwasher so they were nicely dust-free and ready to eat from. Will was just as delighted by the plates and the Christmas glassware as he was by everything else Christmas-related. He ate his pancakes quickly, then hurried off to continue playing with the block tower he and Wyatt had created.

Piper said, "Will's been dying to go see Santa. Want to go with us sometime soon?"

"Definitely. I'm guessing Meadow will come, too?" Beatrice couldn't imagine Meadow *not* going to see her only grandchild visit with Santa.

"I don't think we could stop her if we tried," said Piper with a laugh. "I'll text you a day and time later. He's set up in the park downtown."

Wyatt smiled. "I have some hilarious pictures of myself as a kid with Santa. I must not have been nearly as outgoing as Will is."

"Are you crying in every one?" asked Beatrice.

"Every single one," he said with a laugh. "But my mom kept on taking me every year. Did you two fare better?"

Beatrice said, "I never visited Santa when I was a kid. But I did take Piper."

Piper looked thoughtful. "I don't think I remember any pictures of me crying or looking scared."

"You were pretty ambivalent about the whole thing. Except you always came with a mental list of what you wanted for Christmas."

Piper laughed. "That sounds about right."

After lunch, Wyatt cleared the table and tidied up the kitchen. Piper left with Will. "We always like to leave while we're still having fun," she said with a grin. "But I do think a nap is looming in Will's future."

Will was rubbing his eyes and yawning, so it seemed like a good bet. Wyatt and Beatrice waved goodbye as Piper drove away in the minivan.

Chapter Seven

Beatrice set out for downtown Dappled Hills to check in on June Bug and run her errand for the angel tree. The sun had come out brightly during their lunch and melted most of the remaining snow away, so she decided to walk off her pancakes and their accompanying carbs.

When she arrived at the bakery, Beatrice gave a light tap at the door, not wanting to startle June Bug, who might still be on-edge from the night before. The little woman, who was putting price tags on boxed goods, glanced up. Her face broke into a smile when she spotted Beatrice. She trotted over to unlock the door and usher Beatrice in.

"I didn't want to interrupt you," said Beatrice. "It sounds like you do a lot on Sundays."

June Bug beamed at her. "I'm happy to see you. I have a few minutes before I need to deliver cakes. How are you?"

"How are *you* is more the question," said Beatrice. "That's why I'm here—I wanted to check in on you."

June Bug flushed shyly. "Oh, I'm okay. Thank you for checking. It was a terrible night last night."

"Yes, it was."

"It made it easier that my friends were there," said June Bug earnestly. She sighed. "But I feel bad for Nadia."

"You mentioned you were shadowing her, right? Trying to learn some new things?" Beatrice glanced over at the glass case that was full of all sorts of delectables. "It's hard to imagine that you have more to learn."

June Bug nodded sadly. "I wanted to see some of the fancier stuff Nadia made. She was very good at baking."

"It sounded, from what Liam was saying last night, that Nadia could be a tough person to get along with."

June Bug gave a cheerful smile. "She just worked hard and wanted everything perfect. It made sense." Her gaze clouded a little. "She was nicer than Arabella."

Beatrice raised her eyebrows. "Arabella was unpleasant to you?"

June Bug shook her head emphatically. "Not to me. But to everybody else."

Beatrice wondered if Arabella was another perfectionist, like Nadia was. Judging from the immaculate state of the house, the catering, and the decorations, it certainly seemed possible.

June Bug hesitated, then continued, "She came by a few minutes ago, too."

"Arabella came here? To the bakery?" asked Beatrice.

"She wanted to jump in line," said June Bug, looking uncomfortable.

"Oh. She wanted her own order to come before other people's?" Beatrice frowned. "I'm surprised she needed anything. There were so many cakes and pastries at the party, and it ended early because of what happened. It seems like she'd have tons of leftovers."

June Bug bobbed her head in agreement. "She did. But I also make sandwich platters, if someone asks."

"I see. What did you say?" June Bug was such an easily intimidated woman. From what Beatrice knew of Arabella, it seemed as though she might get totally mowed down by the sheer force of Arabella's personality.

June Bug lifted her head, looking by equal measures proud and shaken. "I told her I couldn't do that. People had ordered days ahead of her. She'd have to wait."

"Good for you!"

June Bug smiled uncertainly at her. "Really?"

"I'm glad you did. She should have known she couldn't expect you to drop other orders to complete hers." Beatrice glanced at her watch. "And here I am putting you behind. I'll let you go. But I'm glad to see you're doing all right. Let me know if you need anything."

June Bug waved as Beatrice headed out the door. Now Beatrice needed to make it over to the drugstore to pick up her items for the angel tree. She'd picked a family and had already gotten the toys on the list, but still needed to get the hygiene supplies and other gift items.

Downtown Dappled Hills looked picturesque enough to be straight off a greeting card. The lampposts had lights strung between them, which looked like a canopy of sparkling stars when it was dark. Each lamppost was wrapped in garlands of evergreen and crimson ribbon, with festive bows at the top. Shop windows were filled with holiday displays. One display featured an elaborate miniature Christmas village. The toy store had gone all out with a large Christmas tree with a display of classic toys like teddy bears, wooden trains, and rocking horses underneath. The bookstore had open books showing pages of traditional Christmas stories.

"Beatrice!" said a peremptory voice behind her.

She turned to see Arabella. Although she must have gotten little sleep last night, Arabella was looking fresh as a daisy. She was wearing a luxurious cashmere coat in a deep burgundy that complimented her fair coloring. The coat was over a long wool dress in a black and white hounds tooth pattern. She'd finished the look with sleek black ankle boots.

Arabella said with a tight smile, "Is there somewhere to eat downtown? I really don't feel like eating leftovers from my party. But everywhere I'm looking seems to be closed."

"It's Sunday," said Beatrice. Her apologetic tone with Arabella irritated her. This was Dappled Hills and most restaurants were closed on Sunday. "There's a restaurant next to the boutique that should be open."

Arabella muttered something, then shrugged. "I guess that's what it's down to, then. Nothing seems to be going as expected today. I tried to get my order from the bakery expedited, and that didn't work either."

"Last night didn't go according to plan either, of course. I'm sorry about that."

For a moment, it was almost as if Arabella wasn't sure what Beatrice was talking about. But then, everything last night *had* gone precisely to plan—the food, the music, the fireworks, the drinks. Everything but the murder.

Arabella made a dismissive gesture. "Yes, you're right. That was a mess, wasn't it? Of all the nights for Nadia to get herself murdered, last night was *not* the appropriate time. Having the party called off after all the planning, work, and money involved was very disappointing."

Beatrice suspected that Nadia would have thought the party disappointing as well. "Did you know Nadia well?"

"Hmm? Oh, not particularly well, no. I knew she was the best at what she did. And she was great about taking direction. She took what I said and ran with it very efficiently." She peered closely at Beatrice, a thought suddenly entering her head. "You're friends with the police chief, aren't you? I think I've seen the two of you talking together before. Rumsey?"

"Ramsay," said Beatrice. "Yes, we're friends."

"Perhaps you can remind him when you see him that I had no reason whatsoever to murder my pastry chef. Particularly at a party I was heavily invested in. As the hostess, I certainly didn't have the time to go around murdering people. I was in sight of somebody the entire time. Nadia's death made life very, very difficult for me."

Beatrice wasn't positive Arabella knew what a very, very difficult life actually looked like. "What did you make of her?"

"Nadia? Oh, she was a truly gifted artist, there was no doubt about that. She was pleased with the direction I provided her. It gave her creativity a set of parameters. Sort of a challenge for Nadia to deliver a pastry with specifications. Of course, she was also an *artiste*, which made for its own issues."

Beatrice asked, "Nadia had an artistic temperament? Did she have a temper?"

"She was very exacting with anyone working with her," said Arabella with a shrug. "Perhaps one of the staff got sick of her and lashed out. There's no telling. I was a bit jealous of Nadia. Talent and youth." She smiled in a self-confident way. "I know I still have my looks, but I have to work very hard and spend a lot of money to maintain them. I have a personal trainer, a personal chef, and I regularly leave town to visit spas. For Nadia, it just came naturally."

Beatrice said, "Everything she made at the party looked amazing."

Arabella smiled smugly. "She was the best. That's why I had her onboard. Nadia has worked at a bunch of events that I've co-ordinated in the past. She always did a fantastic job."

"Did the police give any indication of who might be a suspect?"

"Besides me, you mean?" Arabella's voice was acerbic. "No. They clearly didn't want to share information. But I have my own ideas about who might be a person of interest. And I was sure to let Ramsay know. I'm just not sure if he took it seriously or not."

"Who was it?"

"Nadia's protégé. Liam, I think his name is. I never was all that crazy about him. Every time I spotted him in the house, it looked like he was sneaking around. He just had this very sly expression on his face. Nadia clearly didn't care for him, either. Whenever I was near the kitchen, I could hear her yelling at him for messing up the icing or cooking something too long."

"How did Nadia end up getting saddled with him?" Beatrice knew the answer already, but was curious what Arabella's take was.

Arabella shrugged, looking bored. "I suppose Liam must have applied for the role. She probably thought it was a good idea to get some free help. A sous chef, really. Anyway, Nadia appeared to enjoy feeling like she was important and talented. Having someone following her around, hanging on her every word would do it."

"What makes you think Liam might have murdered Nadia?"

Arabella snorted. "He thought just as much of himself as Nadia did. It was a tremendous clash of egos when the two of them were together. I could tell when he'd storm out of my kitchen that he didn't appreciate Nadia trying to take him down a notch. Liam has a temper on him. I could picture him losing his temper and murdering Nadia on the spur of the moment."

Arabella seemed increasingly tired of the topic, so Beatrice changed it. "I'm sorry I didn't get the chance to see you last night. The party was wonderful."

Arabella beamed at her, clearly enjoying the praise. "Wasn't it? It was one of those events where everything came together super-easily. Until the end, of course."

Beatrice said, "I understand you do huge events like that all the time as part of your job."

Arabella chuckled. "Well, my company does. I don't have to do too much of the hands-on stuff anymore. I've hired some excellent staff for that. In the early days, nearly every part of a party would have been something I was personally involved with. Of course, I'm still incredibly busy. The corporate side of the business is very time-consuming. There's a lot of networking, naturally."

"I'd imagine so," said Beatrice, although she did not know that was the case. "What would you say is the hardest part of your job?"

Arabella struck a pose, looking as if she were searching her very soul for that information. "I'd say firing people. That's the toughest thing. I suppose Nadia and I did have one thing very much in common. Perfectionism. If someone exhibits sloppy work, that reflects poorly on me. Obviously, I simply can't tolerate that."

It seemed like Arabella was boasting about how busy she was and how important. Being in the position of firing people meant she was in a position of power.

Arabella continued, "In fact, I'm thinking I'm about to have to dump my business partner, Oscar. He has a different vision for the company than I do. I bring in clients with my social connections, and he brags all the time about his design talents and the small, exquisite details he adds to each event to make it special."

From Arabella's tone, Beatrice could tell that she thought little about his contributions to the company.

As if to validate this, Arabella said, "The thing is, the events wouldn't even exist if it weren't for me and all the contacts I have."

"It sounds like a big job."

"Oh, it's a tremendous job. But it's very rewarding, too. There are massive corporate events like holiday parties. Then there are charity balls, society weddings. It's a very challenging but exciting job."

Beatrice suddenly had little hairs standing up on the back of her neck. She had the feeling she was being watched. She turned just slightly to see a woman about Arabella's age shooting an absolutely hateful glare at Arabella. Then she stomped off.

Arabella caught the tail end of the look. She shrugged. "Of course, not everyone is a fan. Maybe some people are jealous of my success." She glanced at her watch. "Well, it was good talking to you Beatrice. And now I'll try to find that restaurant you were talking about."

Beatrice pointed out the way to the restaurant again. Arabella thought it through. "Can I cut through there? That will be quicker, won't it?" She pointed to a small alley nearby.

Beatrice nodded, and Arabella strode off. Beatrice headed to the pharmacy, taking out the paper that listed the family's needs, the number of children, the children's ages, genders, and sizes. She'd already picked up the toys the children wanted earlier. She hoped the pharmacy had some of the other things on the list. It was housed in an old brick building with ivy climbing on the outside. The original sign from the 1940s still hung outside, the paint faded but the name still visible. The front window was strung with twinkling lights and featured a small, red mailbox for children to drop off their letters for Santa.

Beatrice had never really paid attention to the non-medical items in the pharmacy before and was relieved to see they had a nice selection of the different things on the Angel Tree list. The parents had asked for school supplies for the kids, along with hats, gloves, and scarves. All those things were in there, and

Beatrice crossed off the items from the paper as she picked them up. Also on the list were usual pharmacy items like new toothbrushes, combs, and nail clippers.

Pleased with finishing the errand with just one stop, Beatrice made her purchases and headed back for the walk home. There were many more people out on the sidewalks than there had been. But Dappled Hills was a favorite stop for people looking for a "Christmas in the mountains" vibe.

Beatrice passed by a stone-paved alley that served as an access point to the main street. It had a staircase that led down to the street below. The steps were made of worn, time-weathered stone and were partially obscured from view by decorated potted evergreens. Then Beatrice stopped. She couldn't tell if her eyes were playing tricks on her or not, but there appeared to be something slumped on the stairs.

She frowned, walking closer, peering around the evergreens. And stopped still when she spotted Arabella.

Chapter Eight

Arabella lay motionless at the bottom of the stone steps, her hair a halo of disarray around her head. The contents of her purse were scattered around her: a lipstick, cell phone, and keys. There was a trace of blood trickling from the back of her head onto her face. Beatrice hurried over to check for a pulse, but there was none to be found. And Arabella's eyes stared blankly forward.

With trembling hands, Beatrice pulled out her phone to call Ramsay. Then she backed off the staircase, making sure she stayed in a spot where she could warn any tourists or locals to stay away to avoid contaminating the crime scene. Because Beatrice had the terrible feeling it *was* a crime and not an accident.

Ramsay must have already been at the nearby police station because he was there in a couple of minutes with the state police. They grimly cordoned off the area.

Ramsay walked back to Beatrice. "You've had a rough twenty-four hours."

"So have you," said Beatrice with a sigh. She glanced behind them at the scene. "I keep thinking this isn't an accident."

Ramsay nodded. "From my brief look, I wouldn't think it's an accident, either. There looked to be a head wound that might have been more consistent with blunt force trauma than with a fall. The forensics team with the state police will tell us more later." He took out his small notebook and pencil. "Can you tell me what happened? Did you just come across Arabella?"

Beatrice nodded. "Although I'd had a conversation with her about twenty-five minutes before."

"Maybe it would be better for you to start from the beginning."

Beatrice did. She hesitated before mentioning Arabella's rant about June Bug. "I know June Bug would never do anything to hurt anybody," she said.

"No, I can't imagine her doing anything, either. But I should ask a couple of questions, anyway. Don't worry, I'll be careful with what I ask."

Beatrice knew he would. But she also knew that June Bug had now been either on the scene or nearby when both murders occurred. If nothing else, she could be a valuable witness to Arabella's state of mind this morning. And if Arabella was being followed, maybe she'd spotted someone lurking around.

Ramsay said, "Did Arabella say anything else of any significance?"

"Well, she mentioned she was planning on firing her business partner. Oscar, I think his name was."

Ramsay's eyes widened, and he made a few notes in his notebook. "How did that subject come up?"

"I'd gotten the feeling that, during our conversation, she was basically bragging about what a big job she has and how important she is. Not in a truly obnoxious way, but just in a fairly obvious one. I think that's why she mentioned firing Oscar—to show how much power she has. Also, she was talking about what she disliked most about her work and firing people was what she came up with."

Ramsay said, "Did she say why she was firing Oscar?"

"Nothing specific. Arabella said something like he had a different vision for the company than she did." Beatrice added, "There was something else that happened. A woman who was about Arabella's age shot her an ugly look. As if something had happened and the woman was furious about it."

"You don't know who the woman is?" When Beatrice shook her head, Ramsay said, "Could you describe her?"

Beatrice considered the question. "She had brown hair that was swept up in a messy bun. She was tall—as tall as I am, I'd say." Beatrice frowned, trying to remember other details. She glanced around as she frowned, then said in a low voice, "Actually, that's her right there."

Sure enough, the woman was standing just a few yards away, watching the police with interest.

"Emily Nash," said Ramsay, following Beatrice's gaze. Then, in a louder voice, he said, "Emily? Could you come here for a minute?"

Emily looked startled, then reluctantly headed in their direction. She cleared her throat nervously. "Hi, Ramsay. What's going on?"

"I'm afraid someone you know has just died. Arabella Chamberlain." Ramsay watched Emily closely for a reaction.

There was one, too. Her face flushed a quick pink. "Arabella? You're kidding, right?"

"I don't kid about things like that."

Emily quickly said, "No, of course you don't. But why? What happened?" She glanced toward the stairs. "Did she slip?"

Ramsay didn't answer the question directly. Instead, he said, "I understand you and Arabella have had some issues in the past."

Emily's flush immediately drained from her features, replaced instead by pallor. "What? You mean—Arabella was murdered?"

Ramsay waited quietly for her to respond. And, after a few deep breaths, Emily said, "Arabella wasn't my favorite person. But I never wished harm on her. Never."

"I'm afraid I'm going to need some details about what your problem with Arabella was." Ramsay tapped the stub of a pencil on the notebook.

"It's not anyone's business. It's long in the past." Emily pressed her lips together tightly.

Ramsay said, "Unfortunately, everything is my business when it comes to an investigation."

"So, it's murder." Emily blinked a few times.

Ramsay again stayed silent.

Emily said, "If you start talking to enough people in Dappled Hills, you'll probably find out, anyway. It's just stupid kid stuff. Arabella stole my boyfriend."

Ramsay lifted an eyebrow. "Recently?"

"No, back in high school." Emily must have noticed the change in Ramsay's expression because she said bitterly, "I told you it was ancient history."

"Just because it's long ago doesn't mean it doesn't still rankle," said Ramsay. "Was the relationship with your boyfriend serious?"

"We were talking about getting married," said Emily. "*Really* talking about it. Like where the service would be, the kind of food we'd have at the reception. We were planning a life together. Then Arabella swept in and took him away." Emily must have thought Ramsay didn't take this act seriously enough because she continued. "It's more than stealing a boyfriend. It's like Arabella stole my *life*."

Beatrice thought that Emily's emotions were now running high. She was so intent on justifying her anger to Ramsay that she'd forgotten she was setting herself up with a motive.

Ramsay seemed to realize the same thing and clearly played the role of devil's advocate. He said in a dubious voice, "So you're saying she messed up your whole life."

"Yes! After Pete started seeing Arabella, I fell into a real depression. She was telling everybody I cheated on Pete. Maybe he even believed it, himself. The whole idea made me feel even worse than I already did. I hated that he would think I could do something like that to him."

Emily looked lost in thought for a minute, reliving it all. "Pete and I had planned our lives together—where we'd go to college, what we'd study, where we'd live after we graduated, and what we'd do for a living. When one domino fell, the rest of them did, too. I didn't go to college because I was having a tough time getting out of bed in the morning. That meant that I didn't get into vet school, which was what I'd wanted to do with my life."

Ramsay said, "Did Arabella and Pete end up marrying?"

Emily snorted. "Are you kidding? No. She just toyed with him for a few months until she got bored. Then she dropped him."

"You couldn't have gotten back together with him then?"

"Of course not," said Emily, looking frustrated. "She'd poisoned Pete against me with her rumors. Everything got derailed because of Arabella."

Emily suddenly seemed to realize what she'd just said. And that, perhaps, she needed to backtrack. She watched as Ramsay kept making notes in his notebook. Emily took a couple of deep breaths to calm herself down. "But Ramsay, this was a long time ago now. Yeah, maybe I'd have been a good suspect if this had happened at the end of high school. But things have changed. It's not the life I'd chosen, but I'm living a good life."

Ramsay said, "But you apparently shot Arabella an ugly look when you saw her."

Beatrice watched Emily's expression, but she didn't seem to realize it was Beatrice who'd reported the ugly look. Maybe Emily had crossed paths with Arabella on other occasions after she'd moved back to Dappled Hills. Emily said, "I think I'm allowed that, don't you? Even though I'm content with my life, it's still hard to forget what she did to me. Look, I'm perfectly happy living alone with my cats. I've turned into a crazy cat lady, but it's not too far out of control. I wouldn't be able to adjust to living with a man after all these years. Maybe Arabella did me a favor in a weird way."

Beatrice thought her eyes said otherwise. And whenever she said Arabella's name, it was in a nasty tone of voice.

"Did you attend Arabella's party?" asked Ramsay gently.

"Of course not!" Emily recoiled. "I was trying to avoid Arabella, not spend time with her. And I would have been the last person Arabella would have invited."

"Had you met Nadia? The woman who died at the party?"

Emily shook her head. "I didn't know her at all."

Ramsay paused. "And although you were so upset with Arabella, furious with her, you had no hand in her death."

"None. Look, I'm not the only person who was sorry Arabella had moved back to Dappled Hills. Nobody liked her, growing up."

Ramsay frowned. "Really? Seems like a girl like that would have been popular."

Emily pressed her lips together tightly. "Yeah, she was *popular*, but no one liked her."

It was an oxymoron of sorts, but Beatrice knew what Emily was trying to say. Just because Arabella was popular, it didn't mean she was well-liked.

"She was a cheerleader, president of the student body, and all that sort of thing. But she bullied people all the time. Arabella was so snobby and thought she was so much more important than everybody else. But she wasn't." Emily paused. "There was someone else who's been just as wronged by Arabella as I have."

Ramsay waited, stubby pencil poised.

Emily looked suddenly reluctant to speak. "I'm not trying to say she did it, you understand."

Ramsay still waited. Beatrice had the feeling that Emily was eager for Ramsay to find another suspect.

"Ruth, Arabella's sister. Arabella has always treated her like dirt. Remember when Arabella's mother's health took a nosedive? Arabella never came back home to help. Ruth was the one helping their mom with her doctor visits and daily care. Ruth works hard. Because she was taking care of their mom, she's never been able to hold down a regular job. The last time I saw Ruth, she said she was working remotely as a customer service rep. After their mom died, Ruth didn't have a good enough resume to do anything else." Emily shrugged. "I asked her if Arabella had helped Ruth out at all, financially. It's not as if Arabella would miss the money, and Ruth did all that work."

Ramsay asked, "Did she?"

"Not a bit. In fact, Ruth said Arabella was very condescending to her because Ruth has never had a big career. She said Ruth 'didn't have vision' or something like that." She paused again. "It's not like Ruth had anything to do with Arabella's death."

Ramsay asked, "Have you seen Ruth downtown today?"

Emily shook her head vigorously. So vigorously that Beatrice wondered if she protested too much.

Ramsay said, "Did you see or hear anything at the party that was unusual?"

Beatrice almost smiled. A trick question. Emily had already claimed she hadn't been at the party.

"No, since I wasn't there," said Emily firmly.

Ramsay nodded. "Okay. If you can give me your name and phone number in case I have further questions, you're welcome to go."

Emily left with relief after giving Ramsay her information. Ramsay said to Beatrice, "Why don't you head home and put your feet up for a while? Want me to give Wyatt a call and ask him to pick you up? Looks like you're carrying bags."

"Just a few things for the angel tree that I'll drop by the church on the way home. I was walking in the first place because I thought it would clear my head." Beatrice gave a short laugh. "I guess it did, but now I need to clear it again."

"I bet you do. I'm sorry, Beatrice. Get some rest, okay?"

Chapter Nine

The walk home was a blur. Beatrice did get out of her fog enough to drop off the angel tree gifts. Then she headed back to the cottage.

Wyatt smiled as she came in and Noo-noo hurried over to greet her. Wyatt must have seen something in Beatrice's expression. "Is everything okay?" he asked, a frown punctuating his brow.

"I'm afraid not," said Beatrice. "Arabella is dead."

Which is when Wyatt hurried over, giving her a hug and leading her to the sofa. "I'm so sorry. What happened?"

"Well, I was walking back with the angel tree gifts and spotted her at the bottom of that stone staircase down the alley."

Wyatt said, "Arabella fell down the steps?"

Beatrice took a deep breath. "It looked suspicious. She had a head injury on the back of her head, but fell forward. I called Ramsay and he and the state police are working on it."

"It seems very coincidental that both Arabella and Nadia, both associated with each other, would die within a day of each other," said Wyatt slowly.

"True." Beatrice paused for a moment, thinking. "I wonder if Arabella might have been the intended target."

"But Nadia was killed in Arabella's kitchen. No one would look for Arabella there during a party."

Beatrice said, "Maybe Nadia found out about the plan to kill Arabella. Then she had to die, too." Her head started hurting, thinking about it. "I don't know."

"Do you want to lie down for a while? Here, let me at least get you a glass of water."

Beatrice said, "I think I'll stay up, actually. There's just too much swirling through my head right now. But an aspirin with the water would be great."

Wyatt returned a minute later with both items. After she took the aspirin and drank a good deal of the water, he put his hand in hers. "Do you want to talk things out? Or would you feel better with a distraction?"

Beatrice immediately said, "I think a distraction is in order at this point."

"I was hoping you'd say that," said Wyatt with a small smile. "I noticed while you were out that our favorite Christmas movie is about to come on."

"*It's a Wonderful Life*?" Beatrice's face broke into a smile. "That sounds like the perfect distraction.

And it was.

Beatrice was surprised to find that she could sleep that night. The old film with sweet Jimmy Stewart had helped her relax. That evening, Wyatt had taken over in the kitchen, making spaghetti and meatballs, his specialty. With the heavy food and a glass of wine, Beatrice had found herself settling down. It was even better when Noo-noo snuggled herself between Wyatt and Beatrice and gave little corgi snores.

She was glad she could get some shuteye because she'd told Piper she'd watch Will for her that next morning. Will's preschool was already out for the Christmas break, but Piper still had work at the elementary school's office. Will was the best grandchild ever, but it required a reserve of energy to keep up with him.

Piper tapped at her door at about seven-thirty. Wyatt had already headed out to the church office. Will came in, bundled up from the cold in a coat so thick that it made it difficult to put his arms down. He was wearing a hat Meadow had knitted, and his little face was flushed from the chilly air and with joy. He said, "Grandmama!" and hugged Beatrice around her legs. Then Noo-noo came trotting up to see him and he plopped on the floor, laughing as the corgi licked his face lovingly.

Beatrice started extricating her grandson from his winter coat and hat. Piper said, "Thanks so much for this, Mama." Then she frowned. "Did you hear the news about Arabella?"

Beatrice somehow felt a little guilty that she'd been at the scene of yet another crime. Her face must have reflected this, because Piper said, "No. You didn't find her, did you?"

"I'm afraid so. I was minding my own business, I promise. I was walking back home from downtown and saw Arabella lying at the bottom of the stairs. I'll tell you more about it later since I know you've got to get to work."

Piper gave her a concerned look. "All right. Are you okay?"

"I'm all good. A lot better than poor Arabella, at any rate."

Piper gave Will a kiss, and he gave her a sloppy one in return. Then she hurried off to work in the school's office.

Beatrice and Will played with trucks for a little while. Then they played Memory, which Beatrice was not particularly good at. Will seemed to have an almost preternatural ability at knowing where the matching card was. Beatrice was basically guessing and not doing a terrific job at it.

Then Beatrice turned on "The Grinch Who Stole Christmas" for them to watch together. Her favorite part was when Will tried to join the Whos when they sang Dahoo Dores. Her second favorite was when Will kept saying *roast beast* and chuckling to himself.

By the time they'd played the game and watched the show, the library was open downtown. Beatrice had decided that would be the best place for an outing. As soon as they walked out of the cottage, though, they spotted Miss Sissy. She was hovering outside, looking cranky, but brightened when she saw Will. The old woman lived within eyeshot of Beatrice. Beatrice was convinced she had a sixth sense that told her when Will was visiting. She absolutely loved the little boy, and the feeling was mutual.

"Sissy!" crowed Will, which was his nickname for the old woman. She beamed at him, giving him a big hug, and pulling a small candy cane out of her pocket.

Miss Sissy gave Beatrice a demanding look. Beatrice stifled a sigh. "Would you like to go with Will and me to the library?"

Miss Sissy was about to leap into Beatrice's car (in the backseat, with Will, naturally), when there was suddenly a jolly toot of a horn. Beatrice turned to the road to see Meadow in her minivan. Now Beatrice didn't bother to stifle the sigh at all. Meadow would, of course, want to hog all of Will's attention. Not that she'd really be able to with Miss Sissy around.

But to Beatrice's surprise, Meadow ended up being extremely helpful. "Hi there, Will! Kiss-kiss! Miss Sissy! Looks like you're all ready to go."

The old woman looked combative. "Library!" she snarled.

Meadow laughed. "No, no, the Christmas craft fair. You volunteered to help with setup today, remember?"

Beatrice had the sneaking suspicion that Miss Sissy had not volunteered at all, but had been volun-told, instead. It happened all too frequently when Meadow was involved.

Miss Sissy continued snarling.

Meadow said in a sing-song voice, "It'll be so much fun! Everyone is going to be there."

Miss Sissy looked pointedly at Will. Will would not be at the Christmas craft fair setup, and he was the only one Miss Sissy really cared about.

Meadow said, "You know how much I appreciate your help, Miss Sissy."

With one final growl, the old woman got into Meadow's car. She waved sadly at Will as she and Meadow drove away, and Will gave her a solemn wave in return.

The library, fortunately, had a little display of Christmas books for children. She picked out Sandra Boynton's *Moo, Baa, FaLaLaLaLa!* and they settled down to read and laugh over the story. That was followed by *Rudolph the Red-Nosed Reindeer*. Will looked very concerned when Rudolph was being bullied by the other reindeer, and Beatrice gave him a hug.

After walking around the library a little and looking at their different holiday displays, Beatrice and Will climbed back into the car. "Church," said Will.

"You want to go by the church on the way home?" asked Beatrice.

Will nodded his small head emphatically. Beatrice knew he loved seeing Edgenora, the church admin assistant, in the office there. She was very good at giving him treats. They could also stick their heads in to say hi to Wyatt if he wasn't in a meeting.

Edgenora was pleased to see Will, and the feeling was mutual. He ran over to give her a hug. She asked him about his day and, with his limited vocabulary, he could still do a great job explaining the Memory game, *The Grinch Who Stole Christmas*, and the trip to the library. She said, "I have a piece of Christmas candy for you." His face lit up as she pulled out a Reese's Christmas tree from a bag.

Beatrice and Edgenora chatted a few minutes about church-related stuff. Beatrice said, "How is directing the Christmas play going?"

Edgenora burst out laughing. "It's absolutely adorable as well as being very frustrating at the same time."

Beatrice grinned at her. "I'm guessing the most frustrating parts are the parents. I still can't believe you were kind enough to take on directing the play, on top of everything you're handling here in the office. You must be Wonder Woman."

"I wish I *were* Wonder Woman. I might handle it better. No, it's been fun, although I don't think I'll volunteer for the role next year. And you're right—the parents can be a handful. They had very particular ideas about casting the play. There was one mother in particular who was dead-set on having her daughter play Mary. She even outfitted the daughter in a Mary costume on the day we were casting."

"For heaven's sake," said Beatrice. Then she paused. "Did her daughter get the role?"

"Naturally! She had a costume already," said Edgenora, chuckling.

"Just be glad Piper and Ash decided Will was too little to play a part. Meadow was dying for him to be in the Christmas play."

Edgenora said dryly, "Yes, I had a lucky escape. That's one big reason I don't want to volunteer as director next year."

"I remember last year the Christmas costumes were looking a little tired out. You're not *making* the new ones, are you?" Hopefully, the answer to this question was no. The last thing the church needed was a burned-out Edgenora. Handling a Christmas play, making costumes, and juggling the admin work in the church office was way too much. At the same time, Beatrice herself had very little desire to make the costumes.

Will was finishing his Reese's candy, miraculously without much chocolate on his face or hands. He watched the fish tank they had in the church office with great interest.

"Oh no, I'm not making the costumes." Edgenora paused. "Actually, that's not completely true. I'm making one of the shepherd outfits. But Meadow, Savannah, and Georgia volunteered to make the other shepherds, angels, lambs, Joseph, and wise men. Oh, and the star."

That seemed like a lot to Beatrice, and Edgenora must have been able to read her expression. "Don't worry, it's not as much as it sounds. Don't feel you need to step in to work on them."

"But it's the 18th of December," said Beatrice slowly. "The dress rehearsal must be coming up soon."

"You know how fast those ladies work. Savannah is probably the slowest, only because she's so very meticulous with her work. But even Savannah has finished several costumes already."

Edgenora straightened up at her desk, looking toward the office door and suddenly looking very professional. "May I help you?" she asked politely.

Chapter Ten

Beatrice turned to see a very thin woman who was almost transparently pale. She had short-cropped brown hair but lovely green eyes that seemed to take everything in.

The woman cleared her throat, looking nervous. "My name is Betty Boxer. This is a little awkward, but I was Arabella Chamberlain's housekeeper."

"Of course," said Edgenora, her expression softening a bit. "What a terrible shock you must have had to hear of her death yesterday."

Betty nodded, a little stiffly. She took a deep breath. "Like I said, this is kind of awkward, especially under the circumstances. But the nature of my job means that, if I'm not working, I'm not making money."

Edgenora nodded. "You're looking for a job here?"

"That's right. I haven't been in town long—I just moved over when Ms. Chamberlain moved back to town. But I really like what I've seen of Dappled Hills, and I'd love to stay here."

"Of course you would," said Edgenora. "And you shouldn't feel awkward. You're simply being practical."

Betty relaxed at this.

"Do you have any references? I know those might be difficult to obtain, considering."

Betty gave Edgenora a crooked smile. "My reference is that my employer, Arabella, kept me on for eleven years. She wouldn't have kept me on for a week if I hadn't done an excellent job."

Edgenora asked, "Have you ever worked in housekeeping for a church before?"

"No, but I've managed very large estates. I'm thinking it might be much the same."

Edgenora nodded and rummaged in a nearby file cabinet. "Here's an application, if you'd like to fill it out and bring it back later."

"Thanks." Betty took the application, gave a small smile, and walked out.

Beatrice looked thoughtfully after her. "I should talk with her for just a moment."

"Why not leave Will here with me? He and I can catch up."

Will said, "Yay!"

Beatrice said wryly, "I think we got our answer. I'll be right back."

Beatrice caught up with Betty in the parking lot. "Betty? Sorry. I was wondering if I could speak with you for a moment. I wanted to tell you I'm sorry Arabella is gone. And sorry for the tough spot you're in."

Betty looked at her curiously, and Beatrice introduced herself.

Betty's eyes opened wide. "I heard you found Ms. Chamberlain yesterday."

Beatrice nodded.

Betty said, "The police didn't tell me anything when they interviewed me. But they seemed to be acting as if Ms. Chamberlain's death wasn't an accident. Do you know anything about that?"

"I noticed the same thing—that they were treating it as if it was a suspicious death," said Beatrice. "But I don't know anything other than that." She kept her observations about the crime scene to herself. She had the feeling Ramsay wouldn't thank her for spreading talk that Arabella appeared to have been struck in the head before her fall down the stone staircase.

Betty said, "I can't believe she's gone. And that the police seem to be treating everyone like a suspect." She gave her a nervous look. "Believe me, I wanted to keep my job. I had no reason to hurt Ms. Chamberlain."

"I'm sure you didn't," said Beatrice.

"I couldn't even give the police an alibi. I was out running errands for Ms. Chamberlain." She shrugged. "It was another aspect of my job."

"Really?" asked Beatrice. "That doesn't seem to fit the job description of a housekeeper at all."

"It did for my job. I was involved in all areas pertaining to upkeep of the house, including grocery shopping and running errands to get supplies for the yard or house."

Beatrice said slowly, "I thought Arabella was running errands herself when she died."

There was a flash of something indefinable in Betty's eyes for a moment. She quickly said, "That was more of Christmas shopping, which Ms. Chamberlain liked doing herself. And she was interested in getting the local baker to do more work for her. I was out preparing for Ms. Chamberlain's business partner to arrive and have a working lunch with her. He'd just driven in last night."

Beatrice said slowly, "So he was already in town." The man that Arabella had said she was planning to dissolve her partnership with.

Betty gave her a quizzical look. "That's right."

"Was Arabella easy to work for?"

"Absolutely. As long as you didn't question anything whatsoever. And I'm the kind of worker who does whatever she's directed to without opening her mouth." Betty gave her a tight smile.

Beatrice said, "I've heard she could be something of a demanding taskmaster."

Betty shrugged. "She wasn't happy, I don't believe. And when you're unhappy, you sort of spread it like a disease, don't you? She had everything anyone could want, but I guess they're right when they say money can't buy happiness. She took her unhappiness out on her staff and other people. I think she was simply frustrated. You had to understand Ms. Chamberlain to work successfully with her."

"What made you decide to reach out to a church this time?" asked Beatrice. "Instead of working for an individual, I mean."

"Originally, I thought I might work for Ms. Chamberlain's sister, Ruth. She's a sweet lady and would be kind to work for. It was silly of me to think she might need someone. I know Ruth doesn't have two pennies to rub together."

"What's Ruth like?" asked Beatrice curiously.

"Very considerate." Betty pressed her lips together before saying, "Unfortunately, Ms. Chamberlain wasn't always the kindest in return."

Beatrice said, "Do you have any ideas about Nadia's death? What did you make of her?"

Betty sighed. "Unfortunately, Nadia and Ms. Chamberlain were two peas in a pod. They both had very high expectations. And the two of them didn't get along very well. Ms. Chamberlain expected too much and Nadia wasn't the kind of person to put up with it. Ms. Chamberlain requested a gingerbread house that was the exact replica of her mansion for her Christmas party. Nadia was a total perfectionist and spent countless hours on the project. The problem was that Ms. Chamberlain kept changing design details at the last minute."

"That would be annoying," agreed Beatrice.

"Yes. And Ms. Chamberlain's time expectations were unrealistic, too. It made Nadia furious to feel that she thought she was slacking off or not doing a good job." Betty paused. "There was something else, too. Something that was kind of odd. Nadia told me someone wanted to kill Ms. Chamberlain."

Beatrice blinked. "Nadia didn't say that someone wanted to kill *Nadia*?"

Betty shook her head vehemently. "No. Nadia never mentioned that she felt in danger at all. But she said she knew someone was going to try and harm Ms. Chamberlain."

"Did Nadia tell Arabella?"

Betty said, "She said she did, but that Ms. Chamberlain thought so much of herself that she just scoffed. Didn't take it seriously at all." She looked at her watch. "I should go. I need to start packing up my things."

"You won't stay in the house in the meantime?"

Betty said dryly, "Well, it's not my place. I think Ruth Chamberlain is supposed to meet with a lawyer soon, and maybe there'll be more information after that. But as far as I'm aware, I'm no longer being paid and no longer have housing." She gave Beatrice a crisp goodbye and headed off. Beatrice walked back into the church and headed for the church office.

There she saw Edgenora was telling Will a fairy tale from memory. Beatrice was clearly walking in on the tail-end of it, considering that the Three Bears had just returned home and Goldilocks was waking in a tizzy. When Edgenora said, "the end," Will and Beatrice clapped. Edgenora took a bow.

"Thanks for keeping an eye on Will," said Beatrice.

"Oh, it was my pleasure. He was a very good boy."

Beatrice gave Will a smile. "Thanks for being good, Will."

"Wyatt?" asked Will.

Beatrice nodded. "We'll go right over to his office now."

Will was very fond of Wyatt's church office. It had swirly chairs that Wyatt let him twirl around in. And he always had mints, too. Wyatt greeted them with a big smile. "There are two of my most-favorite people!"

Will ran over to give him a hug. Right now, Will seemed to have only two-speeds: stopped or full-power. Wyatt said, "Would you like a mint, Will?"

Will did. Beatrice was thinking that after the Reese's candy and the mint, she should probably brush Will's teeth when they got back home.

"Everything going okay?" asked Wyatt as Will twirled in the chair and sang a creative version of "Frosty, the Snowman."

"Oh, it's going fine. Sorry if I seem distracted. I was just speaking with Arabella's housekeeper. She's trying to find work at the church."

Wyatt looked interested. "If she was working for Arabella, I'm guessing she's really good at what she does."

"I'd imagine so. Her name is Betty Boxer. She made a similar comment, saying Arabella wouldn't have kept her around if she hadn't done a good job." Beatrice snorted. "From what I've heard, Arabella wouldn't have kept her around if she hadn't done a nearly-perfect job." She glanced over at Will. "I was thinking there were a couple of things I should bounce off Ramsay. I feel like my head is full of all kinds of theories, but I need to talk them out with somebody."

Wyatt said, "How about if I do a little walkabout with Will through the church? That will give you some time to give Ramsay a call."

"That would be perfect. It probably won't be a long call. Ramsay's got a ton of things going on, I'm sure."

"Take your time," said Wyatt. "We'll go to one of the preschool Sunday school classes, and he can draw with paper and crayons."

Will looked very excited by this idea. He put his hand into Wyatt's, and they headed off with Will chatting happily.

Ramsay answered the phone right away. "Beatrice. You haven't discovered more victims, have you?"

"No, but I'd better knock on wood," said Beatrice. "You know I didn't actually discover Nadia. I was merely in the vicinity."

"That's just a matter of semantics. What's on your mind?"

Beatrice said, "I was speaking with Arabella's former housekeeper."

"Betty Boxer?" Ramsay paused. "You're not trying to run your own investigation, are you? I know you're very good at it, and I appreciate the help. I just don't want anything to happen to you."

"I don't want anything to happen to me, either. But no, the reason I was speaking with Betty was because she was trying to find a job at the church. With Arabella gone, she's not receiving a paycheck. But she's wanting to stay in Dappled Hills."

"That's good to know," said Ramsay. "I do like my suspects to stick around until we make an arrest."

"Is Betty a suspect, then?"

Ramsay said in a tired voice, "Everyone is a suspect at this point. Present company excluded, of course. From what I've heard, Arabella Chamberlain wasn't the nicest to her staff."

"I've gotten that impression, too. Anyway, while I was talking to her, she mentioned that Nadia believed someone was going to kill Arabella."

Ramsay was quiet for a moment. "Is that so? That's curious she didn't bring that up with me."

"Maybe she was just nervous about speaking to the police."

Ramsay said slowly, "So Nadia could have seen or heard something."

"Right. I was wondering if Arabella was really the main target, and Nadia was murdered because of what she knew." Beatrice paused. "There was something else, too. Betty said that Oscar was already in town when Arbella was murdered. You might already know this, but I wanted to make sure I mentioned it."

"Yeah, that was something useful that Betty *did* pass along during her interview with us. Thanks, though. Have you been able to pick up anything else?"

Beatrice thought about her conversation with Melissa Martin. Melissa hadn't wanted her to share salient details of her marriage with Wyatt because she was embarrassed. And she'd said she hadn't attended Arabella's party. Just the same, she thought she should mention it. "Have you spoken with Melissa Martin?"

Ramsay gave a short laugh. "June Bug's crying woman? Yes, we did end up speaking with her. It sounds to me like she had a pretty good motive for wanting Nadia out of the way, regardless of what she says." He sighed. "It feels like the more information I get, the more complicated the investigation gets. I'd like to wrap this case up as soon as possible . . . for lots of reasons, but mainly because it's Christmas. I was hoping to be sitting on my sofa in front of a fire and reading my book. Perhaps with a small glass of eggnog."

Beatrice and Ramsay were reading buddies and always comparing notes on books. He frequently loaned books for Beatrice to read, always encouraging her to try different genres and other authors. He spent a good deal of time writing, too, and longed to retire as police chief and spend his days composing poetry and short stories.

"What are you reading now?"

Ramsay chuckled. "I'm rereading *A Christmas Carol*. I figured a little Dickens would match my current mood. Which is rather bah, humbug. And you?"

"I'm apparently in the mood for a Christmas tearjerker," said Beatrice.

"Wait, don't tell me." Ramsay considered this for a moment. "I'm going to guess *The Christmas Box*. Richard Paul Evans. An oldie, but a goodie."

"Not as much of an oldie as *A Christmas Carol*," Beatrice pointed out tartly.

"True." Someone called Ramsay's name in the background, and he said, "Gotta run. Thanks, Beatrice."

Beatrice walked over to the Sunday school building and found Wyatt and Will playing with Play-Doh. Will appeared to be making a very colorful snowman out of the dough. Wyatt was making a flat Christmas tree with multi-colored ornaments. Will came running over. "Snowman!"

"He's a wonderful snowman, Will. I love him." She drew him in for a cuddle.

"Everything good with Ramsay?" asked Wyatt.

"Yes, he was happy I filled him in."

Wyatt said, "While Will and I were down here, I got a call on my phone from Ruth Chamberlain about Arabella's funeral. Or maybe memorial service. Ruth didn't sound entirely sure."

"I'd imagine the police probably haven't released Arabella's body yet," said Beatrice, in a hushed voice. But Will was back with the Play-Doh and not paying the slightest bit of attention.

"We've set up a time to meet tomorrow morning to talk about it." He paused. "Ruth sounded exhausted, honestly.

"I'm sure she must be. It's got to be tough losing a sibling. Even if they hadn't been very close."

"Weren't they?" asked Wyatt.

"It's hard to say, of course. But I heard Arabella was kind of hard on Ruth. Apparently, she hadn't helped Ruth out at all when Ruth was caring for their mom. Nor helped her financially, even though Ruth lost job opportunities because of caregiving."

Wyatt said slowly, "That's hard. Is it just Ruth now, then?"

"I believe so. I haven't heard about any other family. I'm sure that must make Arabella's death even harder to process. I'll be at the church tomorrow morning, myself—I'm supposed to help water the poinsettias. I'll try to time it so I can speak with Ruth for a few minutes, too, to see how she's doing." Then Beatrice turned to Will. "Ready to head back to Grandmama's house for something to eat?"

Will definitely was, despite the sweets he'd enjoyed earlier. He helped Wyatt put away the Play-Doh, then hurried up to Beatrice, sliding his small hand into hers.

Chapter Eleven

The rest of the day was a quiet one. Piper came by to pick up Will late in the afternoon. Beatrice poked around in her pantry and fridge and was delighted to find she had the ingredients to make one of her favorite quick meals—a garlic chicken rigatoni. While the pasta was cooking, she heated olive oil, put chopped chicken and salt and pepper into a pan, then added minced garlic a couple of minutes before the chicken finished cooking. When Wyatt walked in, she'd tossed the pasta with the chicken and garlic and topped it with grated Parmesan. They'd both gobbled it up as if they hadn't eaten a bite all day.

Wyatt cleaned the kitchen, while Beatrice built a small fire in the fireplace. When Wyatt finished and sat down on the sofa next to her, Beatrice said ruefully, "I feel really tired out, but my brain is going a million miles an hour."

Wyatt put his arm around her. "You've had a lot going on the last few days. It's got to be tough to turn off your mind."

"How about if we work on a puzzle? We got a new one last year, didn't we?"

Wyatt grinned at her. "Not only did we buy a new one, it was a Christmas theme, if I remember correctly." He walked over to the coat closet and reached on the top shelf for a box. "Do we want it on a card table or the dining room table?"

"The answer depends on how many pieces it is."

Wyatt squinted at the box. "500 pieces."

"Oh, that was smart of us! We bought one we can probably put together fairly quickly."

And they did make excellent progress until Beatrice found her brain had finally turned itself off. Well, not probably *completely* off, but off enough to get some rest. She sighed deeply as she drifted off into a dreamless sleep.

Beatrice arrived with Wyatt at the church the next morning. It was a bit earlier than she'd expected because Ruth Chamberlain's meeting with Wyatt to discuss Arabella's funeral was at nine o'clock. She'd slept in a bit, so she felt rushed as she showered, dressed, crammed some toast with jam down her throat, and then hurried to join Wyatt.

Ruth was just arriving at the church when they did. She was a gentle-looking woman with graying brown hair. She seemed older than Arabella by at least five years. She shook Wyatt's and Beatrice's hands solemnly.

"We're so sorry for your loss," said Wyatt.

Ruth gave him a sad smile. "Yes, it is a loss, isn't it? I've had such a hard time identifying exactly what I feel about Arabella's death. I definitely have some anger against whoever took her life before it was time for her to go." She teared up.

Wyatt said, "Let's go inside. That wind is chilly today."

Beatrice pulled a pack of tissues out of her purse and handed several to Ruth. She gave her a grateful smile. "Thank you, Beatrice."

"I'll let the two of you work out the details for your sister's service," said Beatrice, meaning to step away and water those poinsettias.

Ruth reached out and caught her arm. "Would you stay? I'm just not thinking very clearly today and would love someone to help me make decisions."

"Of course," murmured Beatrice.

They headed up to Wyatt's office. Beatrice had always thought it had a fairly comforting air about it. A sturdy wooden desk that had belonged to many previous ministers anchored the room. It had a worn leather chair behind it and two armchairs in front for visitors. There was also the swivel chair Will loved so much during his visits, in case there needed to be more seating. A bookshelf lined one wall, holding well-thumbed copies of *The Book of Common Prayer*, various Bible commentaries, and works by spiritual authors like C.S. Lewis and Dietrich Bonhoeffer. He had a photo on his desk of himself with Beatrice, Piper and Ash, and Will.

Ruth was looking around the room with interest, distracted from her worries for a moment. Then she took a seat in one armchair. Beatrice sat next to her.

Ruth cleared her throat, looking down at her hands, which she'd neatly folded in her lap. "Sorry, my thoughts are just all over the place."

"Take your time," said Wyatt gently. "This isn't a simple thing you're dealing with."

Ruth sighed. "No, it's really not. I didn't expect to have to bury my sister. And now I feel so guilty about how our relationship turned out. I wish I could have been a better sister to Arabella."

"I'm sure she didn't feel that way," said Wyatt.

Beatrice silently agreed. From everything she'd heard, Arabella was the one who could have improved as a sibling.

Ruth smiled her thanks at Wyatt. "We were very close when we were girls, despite the age difference between us. She was always such a pretty thing. I used to play with her like she was my doll. And that's really what she was—a little doll. I do have happy memories of her."

"That's good," said Wyatt. "Those are the kinds of memories that can help sustain you through these rough days."

Ruth bobbed her head in agreement. "Arabella was always so adventurous, so creative. She was forever up in trees wearing a princess dress and waving a pirate sword." Ruth chuckled. "We had lots of happy days until Arabella became a teenager."

Ruth started as her phone rang. She apologized profusely. "I should have put it on mute." Then she glanced at it. "It's Arabella's business partner. I'm so sorry, I should take this. I believe it will only take a minute."

"Oscar," Ruth said in a formal tone. "Thank you for calling." She listened intently as Oscar spoke for a minute before bursting into tears. "Oh, no. No, I'm just grateful. Thank you so very much. Everything is tied up in probate, and I wanted to send Arabella off in the way she'd have liked."

Ruth listened again for another minute. "I'm actually meeting with the minister right now to get some things hammered out for that portion of the service, if that's all right." She listened more, nodding her head as she did. "Perfect, yes. Wednesday would be ideal. See you then. And thank you again so much."

She hung up, eyes glowing through the tears. "Oscar wants to plan Arabella's service as if it were one of their events. He's going to finance the entire thing. I'm so glad."

Beatrice said, "That's wonderful of him." She paused. "This is a rather awkward question, but I was wondering if it was going to be a memorial service or a funeral. That is—"

"You were wondering if the police have released Arabella for burial," said Ruth, understanding immediately. "And the answer to that, until a few minutes ago, was no. I'd called Ramsay, but he said it was up to the state police and their forensic department. So I called them and pleaded with them. I just feel a service would help give me closure. That I wouldn't have such a difficult time wrapping my head around all of this."

Wyatt said, "Did you get far with the state police?"

"Not a bit. They were really giving me the runaround. From what I understand, it was a simple matter of blunt force trauma, so tons of forensics weren't needed, right? Anyway, the state police were talking about red tape and really blowing me off. I wasn't getting anywhere at all. But Oscar just told me he made a few calls and a Wednesday funeral service will be fine." Ruth gave Wyatt and Beatrice a relieved smile.

Wyatt said kindly, "That's great that you won't have to be following up with the police on the phone any longer. That gives you more time to remember those happy childhood memories you were mentioning."

Ruth nodded. "I'm very grateful for that." She rubbed her face, looking tired. "The police have been giving me a hard time in lots of ways. I'm apparently also a major suspect in Arabella's death."

Beatrice frowned. "Are you sure? They might be giving everyone that impression, just to try to obtain information about the case."

"No, apparently it has to do with Arabella's will. Her lawyer was in touch with me last night. He told me Arabella had been quite generous to me in her will. Her son, too, is very well-provided for." Ruth sighed. "Anyway, I'd been out of the house yesterday when Arabella died, so I have no alibi or anyone who can vouch for me. I'd walked in the park for a while, which is something I like doing on Sunday afternoons."

Beatrice asked, "You didn't see anyone you knew there?"

"Not a soul. But then, it was a chilly day in December. It wasn't the most popular time for anyone to visit the park. I was trying to clear my head, so I was sticking to my routine. Sometimes, taking a walk can help me set my mind straight." Ruth paused. "Probably another reason I'm such a suspect is because financial problems have been weighing on my mind. You know how money worries can be; they can really keep you up at night. Now it sounds like all those problems will be in the past. No wonder the cops are looking closely at me."

Beatrice asked, "You'd mentioned Arabella changed when she was a teenager. Did something happen?"

Ruth sighed again. "Arabella's behavior, her daring nature, was so cute when she was a little girl. But when she was a teen, she became more reckless." She quickly added, "It's something Arabella grew out of, of course. In fact, she decided when she was in college that she didn't need alcohol or drugs and quit cold turkey. From everything I've read, that's rather remarkable. But that stint of drug and alcohol use and the people she was hanging out with changed her."

"What did your parents make of the changes?" asked Beatrice. The way Ruth talked, it sounded almost as if Ruth had been the primary caregiver for Arabella.

Ruth said wryly, "They were always so proud of her. She was so cute and pretty. They couldn't see the trouble she was getting into. Or maybe they didn't *want* to see the trouble. I worried a lot about her. Arabella was acting out in many different ways. She totally broke poor Emily Nash's heart by stealing her beau. Emily and her boyfriend had been with each other constantly since elementary school." She looked at Beatrice. "Do you know Emily?"

Beatrice said, "I'm barely acquainted."

"Even so, did she talk about how Arabella stole her boyfriend?"

Beatrice nodded.

Ruth gave a short laugh. "Of course she did. Even if you've just met Emily, she's going to talk about it. It was as if Arabella bewitched the boy. She didn't even care about him; she was simply being cruel. I like to think it was the drugs affecting Arabella and not really her. She strung the boy along and had no intention of being serious with him."

Beatrice asked, "Did Arabella have something against Emily, maybe? Is that why she did it?"

"She just didn't particularly like Emily. Arabella wanted to do something to hurt her. I don't think she realized how *badly* she was going to hurt Emily, though. The girl had set her cap for Pete and planned her entire existence and future around him."

Wyatt asked, "What ended up happening to the relationship?"

"The one between Arabella and Pete? Eventually, Arabella tired of him, of course. He wasn't worldly like she was, wasn't interested in travel, and didn't like a cosmopolitan life. No theater, concerts, or ballets for him. Pete was quiet and more introverted. They really didn't suit each other at all."

"If Arabella was so cosmopolitan what made her decide to return to Dappled Hills?" asked Beatrice.

Ruth shrugged. "Arabella said she missed the town. She'd had such a big life for so long and was on the go all the time that she wanted to enjoy a quieter life again. She'd rather be a big fish in a small pond." She gave a sad smile. "I was delighted when I discovered Arabella was returning to Dappled Hills. I only wish our dear parents could have been alive to see it." A hard look passed over Ruth's gentle countenance for a second.

Beatrice asked quietly, "Do you know if Arabella was having any trouble with anybody? Did she mention any issues she was having?"

Ruth spread out her thin hands. "I wish I knew. The police asked me the same thing. I told them I just didn't know. This, naturally, made them think Arabella and I weren't close." She was silent for a moment. "Maybe we weren't, not anymore. We didn't speak that much, but then, Arabella was always so busy. She was constantly thinking about her business, networking, gearing up her staff for an event. I didn't think too much about it."

"But it sounds like Arabella would have probably let you know if she was having a specific problem," said Wyatt.

"I'd like to think so. I really would. I just don't know. I went to her party, of course. I felt like Arabella looked stressed then. But I wrote it off as Arabella wanting everything at her party to be perfect. Still, she went to parties and events all the time. The more I've thought about it, the more I think she was stressed out about something else."

Beatrice thought about Arabella mentioning that she was going to fire Oscar, her business partner. The man who was now footing the expenses for her funeral. He'd been in town, although Arabella might not have known it on Sunday when she died. "Do you know much about Oscar?" Ruth frowned and Beatrice added, "I just wondered what kind of business relationship they had."

"No, honestly, I don't know him at all. Arabella talked about him sometimes, of course. But it mostly seemed to be related to their business." Ruth paused, thinking. "I believe she did mention the two of them not being on the same page lately, in terms of the events. But you know how partnerships are. I'm assuming they're just like marriages—apt to have hiccups from time to time." She shook her head firmly. "I can't imagine Oscar would have anything to do with Arabella's death. Not after that generous offer to pay for the funeral."

Beatrice wondered if maybe Oscar's generous offer was a way of assuaging his guilt. Perhaps he'd found out Arabella planned on terminating their partnership and acted out of anger. Exactly how long had he been in town? Arabella's housekeeper, Betty Boxer, had said she was out running errands to prepare for his arrival in town on Sunday. Clearly, he'd been there before that.

Ruth continued, "To answer your question, though, about who might have been upset with Arabella . . . I just don't know. It seems to me it must have been genuine hatred that would make someone kill another person. Annoyance at someone doesn't seem to fit the bill." Ruth wavered. "Emily did seem very upset by Arabella's return to town when I saw her the other day. But again, I can't imagine Emily nursing a grudge like that for so many years. And she comes from such a marvelous family. Her parents were lovely people who raised her well."

"You said Emily was upset the other day?" asked Wyatt.

Ruth nodded reluctantly. "She asked me to keep Arabella away from her. As if she couldn't even stand the sight of her. But it struck me as so odd when Emily was at the Christmas party. I brought it up to her, myself. I asked her why she'd attended the party when she'd wanted to keep her distance from Arabella. Then Emily claimed she *hadn't* been there. That I must have been mistaken when I spotted her there. It didn't make any sense. I saw her there, plain as the nose on my face."

"Do you think Arabella would have invited Emily?"

"Certainly not! Arabella wasn't interested in spending time with Emily, either."

Beatrice said, "I suppose Emily didn't want to admit to gate-crashing." Or to murdering the pastry chef, if she'd seen her threatening Arabella. "I was sorry about Nadia, Arabella's pastry chef. Did you know much about her?"

Ruth said, "Oh, Arabella talked all the time about the wonderful pastry chef she had 'on retainer' for the holiday season.

They seemed to have a good professional relationship, from what I could tell. Arabella wanted everything perfect and the young woman appeared to *be* a perfectionist. That would certainly have helped things. Sweets made Arabella happy, and I'm glad she had something to be happy about before her untimely death."

Ruth looked sober again. "I'm sorry I'm taking up so much of your time. I'm sure a minister and his wife have plenty to do in the church less than a week before Christmas. Let's get down to planning."

Chapter Twelve

Forty-five minutes later, the service was planned out, at least Wyatt's part in it. Ruth hurried off to find a venue for the funeral reception and look into catering.

"What are your plans for the rest of the day?" asked Wyatt.

"Well, I'm going to water those poinsettias. Then, I'm contemplating a nap." Beatrice frowned. "Oops. The Christmas party for the Village Quilters is tonight. I'll *definitely* need a nap before that."

Wyatt smiled at her. "I hoped that would be on your list of things to do. Maybe the rest of the afternoon before the party can be quiet for you."

"I do have a bunch of wrapping I need to do. And maybe one or two small things to pick up as gifts. And I should bake goodies for the neighbors, too. But you're right—I need some time to be still."

Wyatt said, "Why not make a list of the remaining things you need to do and then just tackle one or two things every day? There's no reason to knock everything out at one time."

"Excellent point." She leaned forward to give Wyatt a light kiss.

It ended up still being a moderately productive Monday. Beatrice had taken Wyatt's advice to heart and gotten enough done that she wasn't worried about the list of things to do, but not so much that she was worn out again by the end of the day. That evening, Wyatt and Beatrice worked on their jigsaw puzzle again with Christmas carols playing in the background. Soon their puzzle of a cozy cottage with smoke curling through the fireplace and a Christmas tree peeking through the front window started matching the picture on the box the puzzle came in.

Snow was still lightly falling as Beatrice arrived at the Village Quilters' Christmas party, got out of her car, and walked toward Georgia's house. Georgia had a knack for crafting, not just for quilts but for just about everything. She displayed a rustic wreath on her front door, crafted from pine branches and holly berries, and tied with a red-and-green plaid bow. She had mason jar lanterns filled with string lights to light her walkway, casting a warm glow on the snow-dusted path. The porch banisters were twined with pine garland, interwoven with burlap ribbon, and hand-sewn quilted angels.

Beatrice walked inside, and Georgia quickly came over to greet her. "Merry Christmas! I'm glad you could make it."

"Me too," said Beatrice, giving her a hug. "I love your decorations. I'm starting to rethink my store-bought ones."

"You know, it's such a busy time of year for everybody. I cheat and set a reminder on my calendar for the middle of summer. I'm not teaching then and don't have as much to do. It's sort of like Christmas in July . . . I go through my ornaments, toss the ones that are broken, and give away the ones I haven't used in a while. Then I start refreshing my decorations for the upcoming holiday."

"That is absolutely brilliant," said Beatrice, meaning it. "I'm going to try that out this summer. You're right—when I take out my decorations after Thanksgiving, the last thing I want to do is sort through them or make new ones. I *also* don't want to do that when I'm putting the decorations away, which is when the experts tell us to."

Georgia laughed. "The experts and I disagree on lots of things. Come on inside! I've got some spiced apple cider to warm you up."

Not only did Georgia serve hot apple cider, she had quite the spread of food. Everyone asked before the party if they could bring something, but Georgia insisted she had plenty for everybody. On a long table covered with a quilted Christmas table runner, she displayed all sorts of delicious tidbits. There were tortilla roll-ups with cream cheese and veggies, sugar cookies decorated with icing to look like fabric patterns, and fluffy biscuits with a buttonhole design in the center, served with jam. Festive Christmas music played lightly in the background.

Beatrice spotted Georgia's sister, Savannah, sitting next to Miss Sissy on the sofa in front of a roaring fire. She put some goodies on a plate and walked over to join them. Savannah was trying valiantly to have a conversation with Miss Sissy, who appeared to be mainly growling and stuffing her face with food. Savannah looked relieved to see Beatrice approaching. The thin woman gave her a big smile.

"Merry Christmas, Beatrice!" said Savannah.

"Merry Christmas to you, too! And Merry Christmas to you, Miss Sissy."

Miss Sissy grunted at her, which Beatrice supposed was better than a snarl.

"Miss Sissy and I were just talking about the craft fair," said Savannah.

This seemed highly unlikely to Beatrice. Miss Sissy did not appear to be in a conversational mood. It was more likely that Savannah had been giving a monologue about the craft fair while Miss Sissy worked on consuming every crumb off her plate.

"Are you helping out with it?" asked Beatrice. She felt a slight pang of guilt that she wasn't volunteering for the craft fair this year. It was just that Christmas was such a busy time at the church for her and for Wyatt. She'd rather go to the craft fair and enjoy it as a regular visitor than work at the Village Quilters' booth.

"Georgia and I are going to be working the booth some of the time," said Savannah.

"I haven't signed up for anything this year," said Beatrice, grimacing.

Miss Sissy made a cackling sound, and Beatrice looked at the old woman more closely. It almost seemed as if she approved of Beatrice's choice.

Savannah did, too. "You did the right thing," she said in her usual, direct manner. "Christmas is very busy at the church. Plus, you've got a grandson. You need to carve out time for all the things you need to do."

Beatrice nodded, then glanced around the room. There were two Christmas quilts hanging in the living room. One was a modern take on the season, featuring a design of an intricate mosaic of Christmas stars, triangles, and diamonds that came together to form a larger, tessellated star pattern across the quilt. The color palette was a mix of deep reds, forest greens, and crisp whites. "Is that quilt yours, Savannah?" asked Beatrice.

Savannah smiled proudly. "How'd you guess?"

Beatrice hid a grin. Savannah's quilts always stood out. She always favored geometric designs and order. "It's wonderful," she said. "You're such a talented quilter."

Savannah bobbed her head at the other quilt. "That one is Georgia's."

This didn't surprise Beatrice at all. The other quilt was softer, seeming to exude a gentle and inviting warmth. It had appliqued poinsettias, holly leaves, and berries on a soft cream background. The color scheme was a pastel array of blush pinks, mint greens, and buttery yellows. The quilting stitches were curvilinear, swirling around the appliqued elements and creating a sense of motion with the quilt.

"That's beautiful, too," said Beatrice. "I was telling Georgia that I love her decorations. Do you put up decorations, Savannah?" She was curious to find out. Savannah was such a tidy, regimented person. She wasn't sure how she'd feel about the cluttered feeling that decorating could sometimes bring.

Savannah said, "Just a few of those timed candles in the windows."

Miss Sissy made a growling sound, and Savannah smiled. "Miss Sissy was telling me earlier that she's not much of a fan of Christmas lights."

The old woman looked fierce. "Too bright! Loud!"

"I guess you're talking about some of the light shows that a few of the neighbors have," said Beatrice. Savannah looked curious, and Beatrice explained. "There are lights that move or flash along with the beat of the Christmas music."

Miss Sissy made a face. She was definitely a woman who knew her own mind, that was for sure.

The December guild meeting was a little different from the others during the year. No one read the minutes or gave updates on upcoming projects. No one demonstrated a quilting technique, and there was no show-and-tell section where the members showed off their current and just-finished projects. This was purely a social gathering with a secret Santa exchange at the end.

The door suddenly swung open, letting in a swirl of snow and Meadow in a Santa hat. "Merry Christmas!" she said, as jolly as the old elf himself. She'd arrived with Posy, who was much quieter and merely gave everyone a cheery wave.

Miss Sissy grumpily walked off to help herself to more food. Meadow bounced up to Beatrice. "Let's hope this party isn't as exciting as the last one we attended."

"Fingers crossed," said Beatrice fervently. "Have you heard any updates from Ramsay?"

"In what universe do I get updates from Ramsay about investigations? You know how he is. Besides, when he's on a case, he's only home for meals and to patch together a little sleep for himself. She frowned. "Which reminds me I should get to the store at some point."

"Out of food?" asked Beatrice.

"Mm. Maybe. And I'm nearly out of wrapping paper. But I keep forgetting about it."

Everyone caught up, ate, and drank spiced cider for about an hour, then it was time for secret Santa. Beatrice had been relieved to find weeks ago that her secret Santa was Posy. Posy was very easy to shop for. Miss Sissy, on the other hand, would have been very difficult. Unless one was to buy her food.

Which was exactly what a savvy Savannah had done for Miss Sissy. The old woman's face lit up when she opened a gift bag full of delicious junk food. Savannah was a junk food aficionado, and the perfect person to buy for the food-loving old woman.

Posy was delighted by the fabric bird ornaments Beatrice had made. She was a true bird-lover who always fed and housed her backyard birds in birdhouses that her husband, Cork, made.

Georgia had drawn Beatrice's name for the secret Santa exchange, and made a comfy reading pillow for Beatrice. It had a patchwork design with embroidered titles of some of Beatrice's favorite books and a quill and inkwell.

Georgia smiled. "I made a pocket for you to keep your reading glasses."

"How did you know I'm forever laying those down and losing them? Thank you, Georgia, this is so perfect."

After the gift exchange was finished, Georgia got everyone's attention. "Thanks for coming tonight, everybody, and thanks for this guild. The Village Quilters have been like family to me for years."

"Don't make us cry," ordered Meadow, delicately dabbing at her eyes, which had already started tearing up.

"I won't, I promise," said Georgia. "I thought it would be fun for each of us to write a wish for the upcoming year or what you're grateful for from the past year on a fabric square. I'll sew them on a quilt, and we can look at them next year and reminisce."

It was a lovely idea and the ladies all took part. Beatrice, curious to see Miss Sissy's fabric square, peered carefully at it. It appeared she's written both a wish and something she was grateful for. "See Will more" and "Will."

When the women all took their leave and headed out into the light snow, Beatrice's heart was full.

Chapter Thirteen

When she got up on Tuesday morning, Beatrice decided it was time to get out of the house again. Although she often tried to relax and did theoretically believe her retirement years should be quieter ones, she found it difficult to follow through on. A trip to the Patchwork Cottage seemed in order.

Posy had carefully decorated the quilt shop in downtown Dappled Hills for Christmas and it felt even cozier than it usually did. The front window display featured a festive quilt that showcased a charming mountain cottage, very similar to the one on Beatrice and Wyatt's puzzle. The cottage had wreaths on the windows and door. Accents of gold and silver thread gave it a subtle sparkle.

The entrance to the shop was framed by a garland of evergreens and pine cones with a bright red bow at the center. Inside, the Patchwork Cottage was a Christmas quilting wonderland with quilted table runners and wall hangings displaying stars, Christmas trees, and angels. Cheery twinkling lights were strung around the shop. Posy even had a Christmas tree in the corner with handmade quilted ornaments and ribbons. Near the register, Posy had set up a pre-wrapped gift area for any spouses of quilters. There she had pattern and fabric bundles.

Beatrice's smile just from walking into the shop grew as soon as she saw Piper and Will there. Will came bounding up to hug her as if he hadn't seen her in years. "Maisie," he said earnestly to Beatrice.

Maisie was the shop kitty for the Patchwork Cottage. She was technically shared with Miss Sissy, who doted on her just about as much as she doted on Will. She was a beautiful white cat that must have some Persian in her somewhere.

"You want me to come see Maisie with you?" Beatrice reached out her hand, and Will quickly took it in his small one, leading her to where Maisie perched in the sitting area. Beatrice could immediately tell what Maisie's increased appeal was. Georgia, one of her fellow Village Quilters, was fond of making outfits for the cat. She also made pet clothes and sold them online, which supplemented her teaching income.

Maisie was wearing a cozy, quilted Christmas vest that wrapped snuggly around her fluffy body. The vest was a soft red cotton with a subtle pattern of tiny green Christmas trees and golden stars. Attached to the vest was a white faux-fur collar, which gave Maisie the appearance of a little female feline Santa Claus. A tiny jingle bell tinkled softly as she moved to greet Beatrice.

"Isn't she so pretty?" Beatrice asked Will.

Will gave his adorable chuckle and nodded. Piper came over to join them, along with Miss Sissy. Miss Sissy was looking less grumpy than usual, which most likely had to do with the fact

Will was there. She was even wearing a Christmas pin on her baggy floral dress.

Piper said, "School is out, and I've got my break until January tenth."

"Oh, that's a nice long break this time," said Beatrice.

"They'll have to make up the school time somewhere else, but I don't mind. I'd rather have more time off at Christmas. It's just such a magical time of year, especially with Will being this age." Piper said, "I know what I was going to ask you. I was trying to make a list of some of our Christmas traditions from when I was a kid. I'm getting Ash to do the same thing. I thought it might be fun to re-create them with Will."

Beatrice said, "Gosh, I think we had a few of them. We'd always open one gift before Christmas, right before we left for the Christmas Eve service at church."

Piper grinned. "I remember spending a lot of time trying to figure out which present I wanted to unwrap."

"Yes, you were quite a little detective back then. Shaking the presents, trying to see through the wrapping paper. It's amazing nothing got broken in the process," said Beatrice with a laugh.

"I remember we always set out milk and cookies for Santa."

"And reindeer food, too. Remember the reindeer food?" asked Beatrice.

Piper considered this for a second, then her face lit up. "Yes! We put it outside on paper plates for Santa's reindeer."

Will said, "Rudolph!"

"That's right, Will," said Beatrice. "We put out some oats on a plate with red and green sprinkles to make sure the reindeers spotted it."

Miss Sissy looked rather dubious about the reindeer mixture and grumbled quietly to herself.

Piper said, "I think one of my favorite traditions was when you and Daddy drove me around to look at all the Christmas lights. We always had travel mugs of hot chocolate for the ride. That's one we're definitely going to try out. Will absolutely adores the Christmas lights."

Will nodded enthusiastically in agreement.

Miss Sissy's ears pricked up at the pronouncement of Will's love for Christmas lights. "I want lights on my house," she said in a firm voice.

This was extraordinary for a couple of reasons. Miss Sissy had just made her feelings clear about Christmas lights at the guild's Christmas party, and they were certainly not positive feelings. Plus, Beatrice thought it seemed rather late in the season to be putting lights up on one's house. It was December 19th, after all. No one really knew how old Miss Sissy was, but Beatrice had the feeling she was quite ancient indeed. "It's very dangerous to hang lights," she noted in a disapproving voice.

Miss Sissy gave her a snarl in response.

Piper said quickly, "Actually, Dan has a Christmas light hanging business on the side. I saw him advertise it in the paper. You rent the lights from him, and he hangs them up."

Dan Whitner was married to fellow quilter Tiggy, Savannah and Georgia's aunt. He was a general handyman and handled lots of odd jobs. Beatrice had the feeling he could do just about anything.

Miss Sissy immediately pulled out the extremely basic phone she used. "Need his number," she barked. Upon getting it, she proceeded to call and tell Dan she needed the lights done today.

Piper and Beatrice exchanged a look. "Hopefully he's got the time to squeeze her in," said Piper under her breath. She frowned. "And how is Dan even feeling? Is he fully recovered from his surgery?"

"He is," said Beatrice. "Which is a relief to poor Tiggy. It's probably a relief to Dan, too. From what Tiggy was telling me, she was loading him up with all sorts of fibrous vegetables and onerous fruits. It couldn't have been much fun being her patient, bless her heart. And if he's doing Christmas lights as a side-gig, he must be even better than I realized."

Miss Sissy said in a peremptory voice, "Lights."

"Yes, Miss Sissy," said Piper. "It sounds like Dan is going to get to them today, isn't he?"

The old woman scowled at her. "No. Tour of lights."

Piper and Beatrice exchanged another look. Apparently, Miss Sissy was inviting herself along on the ride. That would be Ash, Piper, Beatrice, Will, and Miss Sissy. Wyatt would have to be left back at the house. "You want to come on the tour of the lights?" asked Piper.

Miss Sissy nodded emphatically.

Beatrice repressed a sigh. "Well, tonight's good for me."

"Marshmallows," said Miss Sissy.

"Hmm?" asked Piper.

"In the hot chocolate. Marshmallows."

Beatrice always admired Piper's patience. It was a quality she certainly hadn't inherited from her. "Marshmallows," agreed Piper.

That afternoon, after coming home from the Patchwork Cottage, Beatrice saw Dan busily working in Miss Sissy's yard. It appeared, from all the boxes, that Dan's decorating side-gig encompassed more than just lights. She was curious to see what kind of display Miss Sissy would be having.

Fortunately, it became dark early in December so Will could make his usual 8:00 bedtime with no problems. Piper picked up Beatrice in her minivan. Ash was in the front seat and Will was safely in his child's seat in the back. He beamed at his grandmother as she walked up. Ash said, "Beatrice, here—why don't you sit in the front? I'll get into the back of the van."

"And miss Will's expressions? No way," said Beatrice, grinning. "I'm good in the back." She settled back there and was handed a hot chocolate in a thermal mug. "I'm guessing we're picking up Miss Sissy next?" It really wasn't a question. Beatrice couldn't even dream up a scenario where Miss Sissy wouldn't be part of the group.

"We are. She wanted us to see her house first," said Piper.

"I must admit that I'm on the edge of my seat. Dan was out there all afternoon," said Beatrice.

"That must have cost a fortune," said Ash, wincing.

"I'm sure. It's a good thing Miss Sissy inherited that money from her friend recently. She's not a big spender usually, so she should have plenty of spare cash," said Beatrice.

Miss Sissy's house made all the adults' jaws drop, and Will gave a yelp of delight. The entire façade of the house was covered with what looked like hundreds of twinkling lights, from a classic creamy white to a full spectrum of vibrant colors. The house must have been visible from space, considering how bright it was.

"Look!" said Will with a gasp.

"Boy, I hope Dan has these on a timer," said Beatrice under her breath.

There were life-sized inflatable figures of Santa and his reindeer that appeared to be taking off from the roof. The figures were animated, with the sleigh periodically tilting up, as if it had been caught in mid-flight. There was Christmas music that was synchronized to the lights, making them pulse in time to the music. A nativity scene graced Miss Sissy's front yard. There was also a forest of candy canes incongruously near the nativity, leading to a gingerbread house. A projector cast falling snowflakes onto the house, lending it the illusion of a snowy Christmas night.

"Dan's outdone himself," said Piper breathlessly.

Then Miss Sissy, even more spritely than usual, came dancing out of her house in time to "Jingle Bells." She peered in the van to see Will's expression. He clapped his hands enthusiastically, and she took a deep bow.

"Lights," said Miss Sissy as she climbed into the van. She glared at Beatrice until she surrendered her spot for the bench seat in the very back of the car with a sigh.

"Lights!" agreed Will in a reverent tone.

And there were many more lights to be seen and hot chocolate to be drunk. Meadow and Ramsay's converted barn was lovely, with cascading icicle lights that looked like frozen waterfalls against the rustic wood of the barn. Each one of their windows glowed with LED candlelight. The large barn doors were framed with garlands of evergreen that were intertwined with white lights.

As they continued on their tour, Will crowed with delight, sipping his hot chocolate from his sippy cup. Miss Sissy was just as enchanted. They finally knew the tour was over when Will fell asleep, his cheeks puffing out with little sighs. Miss Sissy had slipped into slumber herself, her snoring much more emphatic.

Piper dropped Beatrice off at home. "How did it go?" asked Wyatt.

"We all had a great time. Have you seen Miss Sissy's lights?"

Wyatt chuckled. "I saw something very bright outside and had to step out and see what it was. I thought perhaps it was some sort of UFO that had landed nearby. It's pretty spectacular."

"I think Miss Sissy wanted to impress Will."

"Did she?" asked Wyatt.

"She couldn't have impressed him more. And Miss Sissy and Will were so excited by all the lights and decorations on the lights tour that they both ended up conking out by the end."

Wyatt smiled. "Sounds like a successful evening. And I'm not going to be far behind them, either."

"Remind me what time Arabella's service is tomorrow?"

Wyatt said, "Ruth decided on a brunch following the service, so it's going to be at nine."

"Early start. I think I might be turning in along with you."

It ended up that the two of them were able to just finish the jigsaw puzzle before they started yawning. The yawning was so contagious that they were both constantly doing it until they lay down and fell soundly asleep, Noo-noo beside them.

Chapter Fourteen

B eatrice, as the minister's wife, had gone to her share of funerals and funeral receptions. She'd seen nothing remotely like Arabella's, however. According to Wyatt, Oscar had flown in an entire team to the closest airport, then had them all driven to Dappled Hills. There was a technical director who was helping to video the proceedings, a florist from Atlanta, a caterer from some other large city, and a band. Beatrice wasn't at all sure where the band had come from, but she suspected it hadn't been close. The reception was being held at Arabella's estate under a tremendous tent.

The funeral service itself was lovely, if also a little out of the ordinary. A famous soprano had been flown in to sing the hymns, accompanied by a quartet. The florist had decorated the entire sanctuary and you could smell the aroma as soon as you walked into the building. There were towering arrangements of white lilies, roses, and orchids lining the aisle and at the front of the church. Each pew was adorned with a delicate bouquet tied with silk ribbons. Wyatt spoke a few words, then there were lengthy eulogies from Arabella's many attendees.

Following the service, everyone drove to Arabella's house for the reception. Beatrice had been a little worried about how they were going to stay warm outdoors on a chilly late-December morning in the mountains. She shouldn't have worried, because Oscar had apparently thought of everything. The tent was actually a grand marquee with sidewalls that closed to create a barrier against the wind while preserving the mountain view. There were patio heaters and ceiling heaters everywhere. And a firepit had been set up for those adventurous enough to stand outside the marquee. Wyatt said, "Wow," in a low voice as they walked in. "Was this what Arabella's party was like?"

"Very similar," said Beatrice. She blinked. She'd never seen such an elaborate funeral reception. They walked into the tremendous tent through a grand entranceway framed by towering topiaries. Inside, the ceiling was draped with billowing white fabric. Crystal chandeliers hung at intervals. There were round tables with Chiavari chairs arranged underneath, each table dressed to the max with fine linens, crystal glassware, and silver cutlery. The floral designers had gone all-out with flowers that echoed the church arrangements—white lilies, roses, and orchids. A memory table near the entrance displayed glamorous photos of Arabella, her achievements, and items reflecting her passions, which seemed to involve travel, music, and philanthropy.

Beatrice said, "I wasn't hungry at all until I walked inside this tent."

Wyatt nodded. "I'm with you. It smells amazing. Let's go take a look."

And the brunch, of course, *was* amazing. There were salmon eggs benedict, quiche Lorraine, bananas foster Belgian waffles, cheese boards, lemon blueberry scones, and a carving station with roast beef and honey-glazed ham carved to order and served with artisan mustards and horseradish cream. On top of that, there was a mimosa bar, along with coffee and tea.

Wyatt and Beatrice filled their plates, then spotted Posy and her husband Cork at a table and walked over to join them.

"Quite a spread," said the laconic Cork.

"You two were both at Arabella's Christmas party, right?" asked Wyatt.

Cork nodded. "It was over-the-top, too. But somehow, this seems even bigger, even though there aren't any fireworks or anything. Maybe because it's a funeral reception."

They all chatted quietly for a little while. Then Wyatt stood to walk over to talk with Arabella's son, Bruce, who'd flown into town for the funeral.

Beatrice said, "I'll catch up with y'all later."

Posy nodded. "I think Cork and I are going to go back for seconds. We'll be here."

Beatrice had seen a tall, lean man who seemed in charge of the entire production. He had salt-and-pepper hair that was neatly combed and an expensively tailored suit that Beatrice suspected was not off-the-rack. He was glancing around the room with an analytical look in his eyes.

Beatrice introduced herself, giving context by explaining she was the minister's wife. "You've done an amazing job setting this up in just a couple of days."

A smile pulled at the corner of Oscar's mouth. "This is nothing. I once had to throw a wedding—a massive wedding—with only a day's notice. I had to call in a lot of favors for that one. I tend to thrive under pressure like this."

"Well, it's all extraordinary. I'm sorry about Arabella. I know you two worked together for many years and I'm sure were friends, too."

A look that Beatrice couldn't immediately identify flashed across Oscar's features. "Yes, it's a terrible tragedy," he said smoothly. "I can't believe she was taken from us so soon." He suddenly frowned. "I'm sorry, weren't you the one who discovered Arabella? I believe the police mentioned that salient fact to me when I spoke with them."

"I'm afraid so. I'm sure she must not have suffered at all, if that's any comfort to you." Beatrice felt fairly confident in saying this. From what she'd been able to observe, Arabella was likely hit on the back of the head. She'd probably blacked out right away.

"I appreciate your letting me know that. I'd been wondering what the end must have been like for her. The police weren't particularly forthcoming with the details. I suppose they want to keep things under their hats as much as possible." Oscar paused. "Am I right in assuming that Arabella must have known something about Nadia's death? Is that why she was killed?"

Beatrice heard a gruff voice behind them. "Making speculations?"

They turned to see Ramsay standing there. He'd come in his suit instead of his police uniform and introduced himself to Oscar. "I'm right in thinking you're Oscar Baldwin, aren't I?"

Oscar gave him a tight smile. "Guilty as charged. I don't believe I spoke with you on the phone, did I?"

"No, I think you might have spoken with one of my colleagues from the state police. They've been helping with the forensics and the investigation," said Ramsay.

"Then you're the ideal person to answer my question. Was Arabella killed because she knew too much?"

Ramsay was careful with his answer. "That's one angle we're considering, but there might be others. I'm glad you're here—I've been wanting to talk to you in person."

"That would have been hard to accomplish, unless you'd been willing to drive to Atlanta. I only came into town yesterday. And only *late* yesterday. The traffic getting out of Atlanta was terrible."

Ramsay's expression looked doubtful. He asked, "Where were you on Sunday afternoon when Arabella died?"

Oscar frowned. "I was resting at my home. Why do you ask?"

"I happen to know that you were here in town on Sunday. Not in Atlanta. That you'd arrived in Dappled Hills earlier than you're saying." Ramsay looked at him with cool eyes.

"That's ridiculous. Whoever told you that is lying."

Ramsay quirked one of his brows. "Whoever told me that is *not* lying. I found security camera footage to back them up. So I'll ask you again—what were you doing when Arabella was murdered? And why were you here in town?"

Oscar pressed his lips together. It looked like he was carefully trying to think up the right thing to say before discarding various options. Finally, he gave a small shrug of resignation. "I came to town early because I understood that Arabella wasn't particularly happy with our business partnership. I wanted to speak with her and hash things out. Like any long-running partnerships, ours has had its ups and downs. I wanted to smooth things over."

"Were you at Arabella's party? When her pastry chef was murdered?" asked Ramsay.

"Of course not. I hadn't even realized Arabella was *having* a party or else I would have adjusted my travel dates accordingly. I knew how high-strung Arabella would be the night of a big event like that one, and the last thing I'd have wanted was to have an important conversation with her when she was under stress."

Ramsay asked, "How well did you know Nadia?"

"Nadia Danvers? I know she was the best pastry chef in the country, bar none. I know she was a hard worker, a creative mind, and a perfectionist in every way. I didn't know her personally whatsoever, only on a professional level. Frankly, I was devastated when I learned she'd been murdered. Her career was only getting bigger. I can't imagine who we'll get to fill her shoes at our different events."

Ramsay bobbed his head. He took out his small notebook and pencil. "Tell me a little more about this business partnership of yours."

"Well, there's not much to tell." Oscar looked impatient. "Really, do we have to be having this conversation here? I should be making sure everything is running smoothly."

Ramsay quirked his eyebrow again. "Oh, I think it's all running extremely smoothly. The most important thing you need to be doing right now is help me figure out who murdered your friend and partner."

Oscar looked somber. "Yes. Yes, you're right, of course. Arabella and I had a great partnership, actually. She was excellent with areas like networking and coming up with ideas for events and outreach. I'm a lot more of a numbers guy and better at doing things like researching and hiring staff. Business has been extremely good."

"I've heard Arabella wasn't happy with your partnership. That she'd spoken about dissolving it."

Oscar stiffened. "Like I said, all long-running partnerships have their ups and downs. Arabella felt she was contributing more than I was. It was just a tiff. What you've heard is erroneous gossip. Arabella and I were planning on expanding the business into the Canadian market and perhaps elsewhere. The future was looking very bright."

Ramsay said, "Interesting. I somehow got a completely different impression. I understand Arabella could be a difficult person to deal with."

"She was simply a woman who knew her own mind. She had vision, focus, and ambition. No one would think twice if it were a man with those traits, but because she was female, people considered them pejorative." Oscar paused. "Arabella did always have a plan and expected things to go according to plan. If her staff didn't make it happen, heads rolled. Perhaps that's why people thought she was difficult to work with."

Ramsay asked, "And how did she treat you? Like staff, as well?"

Oscar looked as though his feathers were ruffled by the question. "Certainly not. We were partners."

"I understand she didn't totally consider you an equal partner."

Oscar shrugged. "You've been misinformed again. Arabella recognized that what I did was just as important as what she did. We often oversaw completely different areas and respected that."

Ramsay made a couple of notes in his notebook. Beatrice thought Oscar, who'd originally seemed cool and unflappable, had a red flush rising from his collar and up his neck. Anger? Or could he be flustered?

Ramsay said, "Do you have any ideas who might have been angry with Arabella? Since you mentioned she could be hard on the staff, was there anyone who stands out to you?"

"Betty," Oscar answered promptly. "I don't know her last name. She's the housekeeper. Has been the housekeeper forever. The last time I saw Betty was when I was visiting Arabella at her Palm Springs home. Betty was sobbing on a bench in the front garden when I arrived. She was complaining about how Arabella treated her."

"Did she mention any specifics?"

"Sure," said Oscar. "Lots of them. Betty was rarely allowed personal days off, for one. And she said Arabella often treated Betty more as part of the furniture than an actual human being. She didn't engage in much conversation with her. Betty apparently spent tons of time meticulously caring for Arabella's extensive wardrobe and was never thanked or complimented. Betty said she felt micromanaged, too, because Arabella would double-check the work she'd completed and made her go back and redo some of it."

Beatrice winced. Arabella sounded like a horrible, exacting employer.

Ramsay must have thought the same, judging from his expression.

"Worst of all," said Oscar, "Betty basically raised Arabella's son, Bruce. He's a great guy, probably because Betty spent so much time with him. Arabella was often away, building the business when he was small. Arabella never gave Betty any sort of recognition for that. And now Bruce is in college on the other side of the country, and Betty misses him."

Ramsay nodded. "How about the apprentice pastry chef? Liam? Do you know him?"

Oscar shook his head. "He came along with Nadia, so I didn't know him. He *is* helping out today, though. A local coordinator called him in to help with the pastries we have here at the reception." He looked suddenly impatient. "And if that's it, I really should go supervise to ensure everything is going well."

Chapter Fifteen

Ramsay got the information for where Oscar was staying in town and then let him go. He looked thoughtful as he watched Oscar walk away. "Yeah, that guy hasn't been totally upfront with us."

"I'm guessing that's a skill he might have honed in the business world," said Beatrice.

"I had the feeling I wasn't going to get too much information out of him." He sighed. "Anyway, on to other things. Could you do something to distract Meadow for me? She's about to drive me out of my mind."

Distracting Meadow was about the last thing on Beatrice's mind, but she'd like to help Ramsay out if she could. "What's going on with Meadow?" She glanced around. "Come to think of it, I don't think I saw her at the funeral or here at the reception."

"That's the thing. She's got this Christmas craft fair on her brain 24/7. It's like she's hyper-focused on it or something." Ramsay rubbed his ever-growing forehead tiredly.

"She must be bad," said Beatrice. "You're really not home at all right now, are you? With two murders, I mean?"

"That's precisely how bad she is. I'm only home to grab food or a little sleep. There hasn't been any food in the house to speak of and her cooking is non-existent." Ramsay looked very sorry for himself.

Beatrice couldn't resist the opportunity to tease him. She rarely got the chance. "It sounds like you've *both* been very busy. I'm sure you could scrounge up some frozen waffles or something."

"No, I mean she hasn't even been to the *store*. There's like some olives and mozzarella cheese and that's about it. We're even low on breakfast cereal." Ramsay's face was glum.

That did sound pretty dire. Meadow always had a fully stocked kitchen, and cooking was one of her favorite pastimes, something Beatrice had taken advantage of more than once. Cooking was certainly not one of *Beatrice's* favorite pastimes. She was lucky Wyatt was happy to share the cooking duties.

"Tell you what," said Beatrice. "How about if I see if Piper and Will want to go visit Santa Claus. Piper was talking to me about it just recently."

Ramsay's face lit up. "Oh my gosh, that would make Meadow's day. And mine, by proxy."

Beatrice said, "I'm sure there are plenty of volunteers helping with the craft fair. It's not like they're not going to pull it together without Meadow helping out all day every day."

"You know how Meadow is," said Ramsay. "When she volunteers for something, she goes all in. It's actually a very admirable trait . . . unless there's no food in the house." He flushed. "I do know how to go to the grocery store, of course. But by the time I've been making it home at night, the store is already closed."

"Well, seeing Santa will help for today, anyway. I'll remind Meadow to stop by the grocery store and restock. Maybe taking a day off from helping will reset her and make her go back to normal Meadow."

"Fingers crossed," said Ramsay fervently. "And, if you'll excuse me, I'm going to go load up a plate with that delicious-looking food." He walked off, looking ravenous and also just the slightest bit grouchy. Being hungry wasn't particularly good for anyone's disposition.

Beatrice had spoken with Ruth and Arabella's son, Bruce, at the funeral. Now she was interested in speaking with Liam, Nadia's apprentice pastry chef again, since Ramsay had just mentioned him. She looked over at where the pastries were, but they seemed well-stocked. Liam was unlikely to keep putting more out there. So she looked outside the marquee tent, where she saw Liam smoking a cigarette and looking bored.

He rapidly stomped out the cigarette when he saw her approaching, but then looked at Beatrice more closely and recognized her. "You were on the scene when we found Nadia," he said.

"That's right. I'm Beatrice. Liam, isn't it?"

He nodded, looking bored again.

"I'm surprised you're still in town," said Beatrice. "I'd have thought Arabella would have let you leave after the party."

"Yeah, well, the cops didn't want me to leave town. That wasn't easy to swing, considering I don't have any income coming in." Liam shrugged. "At least I was able to work this gig."

The gig being Arabella's funeral reception. He must have realized how he sounded, because he quickly said, "I didn't mean it like that. I'm just glad to have a little money. Hotel rooms aren't free."

Beatrice was about to ask him a few gentle questions about his thoughts on Arabella's death when Liam was suddenly called away by someone with an apron and an irritated expression. "Gotta go," he said under his breath.

Beatrice walked back inside the tent and looked for Wyatt. Fortunately, it seemed like he was wrapping up his time at the reception. "Ready to head out?" he asked.

"I think so, if that's okay. Ramsay asked if I could distract Meadow this afternoon." Beatrice made a face.

They walked toward Wyatt's car. "An assignment from Ramsay," he said.

"Yes. And not the easiest assignment in the world. It sounds like Meadow has gotten herself completely wrapped up in the craft fair stuff, to the detriment of Ramsay's nutrition."

Wyatt chuckled. "He's hungry."

"Right. My job is to invite Meadow to see Santa." Beatrice looked out the passenger window, trying to think of the logistics of who should go. Maybe just Piper, Meadow, Will, and herself for this one. It would be a zoo if Ash and Wyatt came along.

"Don't you think Meadow is a little old to see Santa?" asked Wyatt lightly.

Beatrice frowned, then laughed. "I meant that I would invite Meadow to see *Will* meet Santa. And I can't possibly imagine a world where Meadow would turn down that offer."

When they got back home, Beatrice let Noo-noo out, then called Piper. Piper said Will had a lovely nap that afternoon and should be in high spirits to meet the jolly elf. They picked a time to meet at the square downtown. Beatrice said she'd pick up Meadow and see them there.

As expected, Meadow was overjoyed at the idea of seeing Will visit Santa downtown. "Wonderful!" she said. "Oh, how fun. Yes, I'll be there."

"You're sure you don't have any craft fair stuff to do?" asked Beatrice with a small smile.

"Are you kidding? Nothing is more important than my darling grandson. When are you picking me up?"

It wasn't long before Meadow was climbing into Beatrice's car. "So exciting!" said Meadow. "I can't believe what a big boy Will is."

Beatrice said, "I hope Santa is especially good with kids. I remember taking Piper to see Santa when she was little. She was not at all amused with him. It resulted in some pretty hilarious pictures. Hilarious *now*, anyway. They weren't funny at the time."

"Will is going to love it. He's such a big, brave boy. I'm so glad you called me up!" Meadow chatted the entire short drive to the square downtown. When she started talking about all the craft fair details, Beatrice felt she should intervene.

"What kinds of things did you get from Santa when you were a little girl?" she asked Meadow.

"Gracious, what a fun thing to remember! Let's see . . . I remember getting a Chatty Cathy doll. Oh, they were so much fun. My best friend and I used to have Chatty Cathy tea parties until my parents made us take the dolls outside."

"Too much talking, I'm guessing," said Beatrice.

"That's right. Lots of 'I hurt myself,' and 'Please take me with you,' and 'I love you.' But she was a darling thing. What about you?"

Beatrice considered this. "I think I liked my Etch-a-Sketch the best. Or my Spirograph."

"Of course you did! Those forecasted your future interest in art. No wonder you ended up an art museum curator."

Beatrice wasn't quite sure there was much of a connection between her odd, blocky Etch-a-Sketch creations and the folk art she curated, but she smiled and nodded just the same.

Meadow said, "I forgot about my Easy-Bake Oven! That was the best. I baked in that little thing all the time."

"And now look at you," said Beatrice. "You're a cooking wunderkind." She felt she was doing a great job both distracting Meadow from the craft fair and reminding her how much she enjoyed baking and cooking. Which she did. She was forever telling Beatrice how much she loved it.

"Goodness, that reminds me. We've got something of a crisis going on with the craft fair food committee right now. We had a major vendor cancel on us at the eleventh hour. I mean, the craft fair is Friday, for heaven's sake. We're trying to find someone to fill in, but it's been very difficult this close to Christmas."

Beatrice could see what Ramsay meant. It was tough to redirect Meadow. She was like a homing pigeon returning to the same topic.

"You know, that's what the folks who are paid members of the committee need to figure out. Remember, you're volunteering. You don't need to take on all that stress. The important thing is spending time with your family."

Meadow gave her a smile. "You're absolutely right, Beatrice. I need to be focused on Will this Christmas. He's old enough now to really enjoy everything . . . church, the Christmas trees, Santa."

Beatrice thought wryly that she'd rather have Meadow focus more on Ramsay than Will. Sharing Will on holidays could be a difficult proposition. At least she was talking about a different subject.

The square downtown was beautifully outfitted with a grand Christmas tree that towered high with twinkling lights and shimmering ornaments. Santa's chair, which looked more like a throne, was right in front of the tree with a red carpet leading up to it. Poinsettias sat around the chair and lined the walkway leading up to Santa. Christmas music was piped in and played from a speaker.

Will was beside himself, he was so excited. He ran up to hug his grandmothers. "Look! Santa!" he said.

"He's wonderful, isn't he?" asked Meadow.

Will nodded enthusiastically. He looked especially adorable in a toddler-sized Christmas sweater that displayed a knitted Santa Claus with a fluffy beard.

"Let's get in line," said the ever-practical Beatrice. "It might take us a few minutes to see him up-close."

An elf greeted them, took down their information, and provided Piper with a price sheet for the photography. Then she gave Will a candy cane. There was a small table nearby with coloring books and crayons in case any of Santa's small visitors wearied in line while waiting to see him.

Will, however, seemed totally amused watching the proceedings. He smiled as each child spoke with Santa and left with a small toy or book provided by one of the elves. Beatrice was relieved that no one whatsoever was crying. Perhaps that was because of Santa, who seemed absolutely wonderful and a total pro. Beatrice had always felt crying had a domino effect for children and was delighted the kids were all so happy.

When it was Will's turn, he practically skipped up to see Santa. He sat on Santa's lap and appeared to be having a very warm conversation with him.

"See?" demanded Meadow. "He's remarkable. I keep telling you that."

Piper and Beatrice exchanged grins. They thought Will was remarkable too, but Meadow seemed to think he was the next Einstein.

Then Will told Santa what he'd like in his stocking, which included a fire truck with a bell, sidewalk chalk, and boats for the bathtub. Meadow discreetly took notes. "Just to make sure Santa gets everything he wants," she explained to Piper.

Will happily left with a book about Rudolph. Then he gave Meadow and Beatrice the inside scoop on what Santa was like. "Great!" was Will's opinion.

Piper said, "I have a couple of errands to run with Will real quick while I'm downtown."

"We'll watch him for you," said Meadow immediately.

Beatrice was more than happy to watch Will, too. Although she thought her Meadow quota was almost full. But she was willing to deal with more Meadow to spend time with Will.

Piper and Beatrice switched cars, so Beatrice had the child seat. Then Beatrice drove them all to her house.

Will was very thoughtful on the way back to Beatrice's. "Sissy?" he asked.

Meadow sighed. Beatrice was sure the last thing she wanted was to share Will with anyone else. "You want to see Miss Sissy?"

"Giff present."

Meadow smiled at Beatrice. "Isn't that so sweet? Will wants to give her a present."

Beatrice said, "The only problem is that we don't have one for him to give her."

"Giff present."

Beatrice said, "Would you like to make a drawing for Miss Sissy? I don't think her fridge has any drawings at all on them."

Will looked faintly scandalized at the idea of a bare fridge. He nodded.

"Great idea!" said Meadow.

Back at Beatrice's cottage, she pulled out some white paper from the printer and some crayons, putting them on the table.

"What are you going to draw?" asked Meadow with interest. "Santa? Christmas trees? Presents?"

Will shook his head. "Me and Sissy."

Meadow put her hand to her heart and gave Beatrice a look. "That's so sweet."

Will spent a long time on the drawing. He was at the age where kids mostly just filled in the lines instead of making many of their own. He carefully drew a lopsided circle to indicate himself, with spindly sticks for legs and arms and two dots for eyes. He did the same for Miss Sissy, making her a somewhat taller, lopsided circle. He had their stick arms holding hands.

"All done?" asked Beatrice. "That's a beautiful drawing." And there was no question Miss Sissy was going to love it.

Will nodded. "Giff present."

They walked across the street to the old woman's house. Will looked with great interest at her inflatables, which were slumped on the ground until the nighttime light show started up.

Meadow said, "Want to ring her doorbell, Will?" She gave the boy a little lift so he could reach it more easily.

Miss Sissy came stomping to the door and opened it, looking quite fierce. Her scowl quickly melted away, however, when she saw Will in front of her, still wearing his adorable Santa sweater.

"Giff present," said Will with a grin. He had his hands with the picture behind him. He brought the picture around and Miss Sissy beamed at him. "You 'n me," he said.

Which was when Beatrice saw tears spring to Miss Sissy's eyes as she studied the lopsided circles that were hand-in-hand.

"Fridge," said Will solemnly.

Miss Sissy looked confused, and Meadow quickly stepped in to translate. "Will thinks the picture would be best displayed on your fridge."

Beatrice put her hand out. "I've brought a couple of magnets, in case you didn't have any."

Miss Sissy reached out her hand for them. "Fridge," she said to Will, nodding.

A car suddenly pulled into Miss Sissy's driveway, and she snarled. It was Piper, in Beatrice's car. She waved cheerfully. "All done with my errands. Hi, Miss Sissy!"

Miss Sissy muttered under her breath in response, clearly not happy to see Piper there to whisk Will away.

Meadow said, "I've got to run, too. The craft fair is Friday! Can you believe how quickly time has flown? There's a lot to do still. But this was a wonderful break." She swooped down to plant a kiss on Will's cheek.

Beatrice quickly said, "Hey, remember, you asked me to remind you to go to the store to pick up some food for you and Ramsay."

"Did I?" asked Meadow vaguely. "How extraordinary of me! I don't remember that at all. But, come to think of it, I don't believe we have much to eat at all. And I desperately need more Christmas wrapping paper."

"We have gobs of wrapping paper, so if you forget, just run by."

"Thanks, Beatrice! But I really should remember it. I'll go home for a second, then hop in the car." And she hurried away.

Beatrice said, "We'll see you soon, Miss Sissy. We all loved your light show last night." Especially since Dan *had* put the lights on a timer and everything had shut off by ten o'clock.

Miss Sissy grunted in response, then gave Will a tender hug, which he returned. Then Beatrice and Will walked back across the street so Piper could take her minivan back and get back home to wrap presents.

Chapter Sixteen

Thursday ended up being a blessedly quiet day. Beatrice spent the day quietly finishing up Christmas chores, doing a bit more wrapping, reading her book, and walking Noo-noo. The craft fair's opening was at five o'clock Friday evening, and it ran through Sunday afternoon. Wyatt and Beatrice headed out before five on Friday in the fond thought they might beat the crowds at the fairgrounds. Unfortunately, this was not the case, and they struggled to find a parking spot, despite the massive gravel lot.

"This is great for the vendors," said Wyatt, always one to look at the bright side. "Hopefully, they'll get lots of sales."

The fairgrounds were laid out with booths draped with lights and greenery. From the map they had, the vendors sold everything from handmade jewelry and wood-carved toys to scented candles and artisanal soaps. And quilts, of course. Which needed to be Beatrice's first stop.

"I'm surprised you didn't want to contribute a quilt this year," said Wyatt as they walked over to the Village Quilters booth.

"No, I thought that I'd take a break this year. Try to take things a little easier."

Wyatt nodded. "Good idea. It sounds like Meadow might want to consider doing the same next year, from what you were telling me."

"It would be *good* for her to take a break, but it's very unlikely. You know Meadow—she loves to stay busy."

But Beatrice knew she really didn't have room to talk. After all, she was the one who'd found the slower pace of retirement difficult to adjust to. And she had a very tough time sitting still.

The Village Quilters booth was filled with quilts with all sorts of Christmas patterns—poinsettias, stars, nativities, and snowflakes—displayed on racks and hung from the sides of the booth. There were smaller items like quilted ornaments, table runners, and placemats on tables inside the booth. A miniature Christmas tree decorated with quilted ornaments stood in one corner.

"Hey there!" said Meadow, excitedly greeting Beatrice and Wyatt as if she hadn't seen them for years. "Doesn't everything look great?"

Wyatt said, "You've done a fantastic job putting the craft fair together, Meadow. It's obviously a tremendous success, too. The parking lot was nearly full."

Meadow looked smug. "It's sort of like that movie. *If you build it, they will come.*"

Beatrice wasn't at all sure that a craft fair compared to a baseball field inhabited by the ghosts of great players. But she nodded and smiled, along with Wyatt.

Meadow said, "Piper said she and Ash will be here with Will soon. I told her to be sure to take Will to Santa's workshop, where he can make crafts. But I forgot to tell her about all the other stuff for kids." Meadow made a face. "I've been so caught up with organizing this thing that my mind is all over the place."

"If we see Piper and Ash before you do, we'll be sure to tell them," said Beatrice. "What are the other activities?"

"Gracious, there are tons of them. There's a face painting booth where Will can get a Christmas tree or snowflakes on his face. There's another booth that has puppet shows and hand-made puppets for sale. There's cookie decorating at June Bug's booth, and you know those cookies will be delicious. Oh, and there's a guy making balloon animals into reindeer." Meadow frowned. "I'm sure I'm forgetting something. There are games somewhere, I think."

"That's a lot of activities for kids this year," said Wyatt, sounding impressed. "I don't remember there being all that much last year."

"Right?" asked Meadow. "That's what I said, too. I told the organizers that more families would show up and spend money if there were things for their little guys and gals to do. And I think that's exactly what's happening."

There did seem to be lots of families with young children around, noted Beatrice. She said, "Thanks for the overview. Wyatt and I are going to make a lap around the fair and take it all in."

"And visit June Bug's booth," said Wyatt with a grin. "I definitely want to get over there before her famous Christmas pudding is sold out."

"Oh my gosh, yes," said Beatrice. "Wyatt and I got the last one last year and had to split it. I was licking the spoon by the end."

Meadow said, "Hey, I want some Christmas pudding, too! I didn't realize that was a thing. What's in it? I'm guessing, since June Bug made it, that it's not just chocolate pudding with red and green sprinkles on it."

Wyatt said, "I don't know what's in there, but it's delicious."

Beatrice weighed the question carefully. "When I describe it, it's not going to sound like much. But believe me when I say it's the best thing you ever put in your mouth. She's got brandy-soaked fruits—raisins, dates, and currants. But she has some brighter ingredients in there, too." She looked at Wyatt.

"That's right. Candied oranges, maybe?"

Beatrice nodded. "Exactly. And she adds spices. Cinnamon, nutmeg, and ginger. Maybe cloves, too."

"And the pudding is sweet," said Wyatt. "I think it must have brown sugar in it. Or molasses."

"Or both," said Beatrice.

Meadow said, "Can you pick up one for me, too? Here's some money." She stuck her hand in a patchwork purse and retrieved ten dollars. "I'm stuck at this booth until Savannah and Georgia arrive to relieve me. But I do want some Christmas pudding before she runs out!"

"I'll bring some back to you," promised Wyatt. But then he started looking closer at a gorgeous Christmas quilt featuring a snow-covered village, complete with tiny appliqued houses with embroidered wreaths and smoke rising from their chimneys. Meadow fussed sternly at him. "Wyatt, hurry! I don't want to miss out."

Wyatt scrambled away with Beatrice, who was chuckling. "I think we must have over-sold the pudding to her. Now you'll have to race back to the quilting booth to hand it over."

Wyatt grinned. "Yeah, we might have gotten her a little too excited about it. But I don't mind. It sounds like she deserves a treat after all the hard work she's been putting into setting all this up."

June Bug had carefully decorated her booth to catch the eye of the roving fairgoer. It sported a gingerbread theme with faux candy decorations. The lettering on her sign looked like icing and there were gumdrops painted around the letters. On tiered stands, she displayed Christmas cookies, gingerbread houses, fruitcakes, and assorted pastries, all wrapped in clear cellophane with red ribbons.

Wyatt looked slightly panicky. "I don't see any puddings."

June Bug stared at him with alarm. Perhaps she'd never seen the mild-mannered minister looking so flustered.

Beatrice gave June Bug a big smile. "Hi June Bug! Merry Christmas. You might not know this, but Wyatt is a huge fan of your Christmas puddings. We don't see any out—are there some in the back?"

June Bug gave a quick smile in return before trotting over to a thermal bag. "I have to keep them in here with dry ice to keep them cool."

Wyatt relaxed in relief. "That's great news, June Bug. Thank you. They're delicious. Could we have three? Meadow wants to try one, too."

June Bug nodded and dove into the bag to pull them out.

"Maybe we should come back to the fair tomorrow with a thermal bag of our own," said Beatrice.

"That," said Wyatt emphatically, "is a great idea."

A large family came into the booth behind them, the kids gaping at all the treats on the tiered stands. June Bug quickly checked out their puddings, gave them a cheery wave, and started helping the family with what sounded like a large order.

"I'll take this back to Meadow," said Wyatt. "Why don't you take a seat over there on that bench? It looks like we'll be doing lots of walking tonight, and you've had a busy week."

Beatrice didn't need much persuading. She plopped down on the bench and looked at the scene around her. There were lots of families this year, as Wyatt had mentioned earlier. Some of them were clutching reindeer balloon animals, others were munching on what looked like June Bug's Christmas cookies.

Then she spotted Liam, the apprentice pastry chef, wandering through the fair, peering into various booths. His dark hair was studiously unkempt, and he had a slight smile on his face as he surveyed the small-town fair.

Beatrice hesitated, then called out to him. Liam turned in surprise, then walked toward Beatrice.

"Hey," he said with a smirk. "It seems like you're everywhere right now."

"Or you are," said Beatrice.

Liam shrugged. "Well, I'm bored out of my mind. Nothing against Dappled Hills, believe me. It's totally a place I'd want to retire to one of these days. I love the mountains and stuff. It's just a small town . . ." He paused, ". . . A very small town."

His expression turned serious as his gaze followed a cop in uniform—Ramsay's deputy. He sighed as the officer passed by him, but still looked jittery. "The cops are asking me lots of questions. They need to get off my back. I barely even knew Arabella."

"Were you able to give them an alibi for Arabella's death?"

"Nope," said Liam. "And you know I was right on the scene when Nadia croaked. The cops have got it in for me, I'm telling you. I don't have an alibi for Arabella's death because I was sleeping in that morning."

Beatrice noted it had hardly been morning when Arabella died. It was early afternoon. But Liam was still a very young man, and she remembered how long young people could sleep.

Liam must have read Beatrice's mind because he made a face. "Yep, I know it was late to wake up. I was up late Saturday night playing video games, so I was just catching up on my sleep. I wasn't out murdering anybody. I was just happy to have a break, you know? Ever since I started my internship with Nadia, it's been go, go, go. Nadia was always in demand, so we were traveling everywhere. Now I've got a few days off."

"What are you going to do about your internship?"

Liam shrugged again. "The school is trying to place me in another spot. Fingers crossed. I've put too much time and money into school to have everything fall apart now. It doesn't help that I'm apparently a suspect in a murder investigation. The cops have to be stupid if they think I killed Nadia or Arabella. I mean, Nadia was the one who was helping me get to a level where I can be on my own two feet: to be a top pastry chef for a major restaurant or for catering. Why would I do anything to mess that up?" he demanded.

Beatrice shook her head. "I'm sure the police are just following procedure. I wouldn't worry about it."

But Liam still brooded. He must not have been in the mood to prevaricate, or perhaps he simply wanted to talk things out. He said, "The problem is I wasn't crazy about Nadia. I'm sure the cops have picked up on that. Plenty of people saw me gritting my teeth when Nadia was around. We did argue a lot."

"What about?"

Liam said, "Small stuff. Basically, artistic differences. I know it sounds crazy that I was arguing with the best pastry chef around when I don't have much experience. But the idea with the internship is that Nadia was supposed to help me find my way and figure out my own path. Let me create masterpieces or total trash. *Learn* from the experience."

"Nadia didn't let you take over the helm?"

Liam looked puzzled, as if he didn't understand the expression. He said slowly, "Well, she didn't let me do as much as she should. Nadia had this stuffy, boxed-in idea of how desserts should be. I had a totally different concept: more modern, fresher. I spend a lot of my spare time experimenting with food. I love it—it's sort of a science experiment or like I'm a mad scientist or something. Sometimes I got the impression Nadia didn't even *enjoy* what she was doing. Was she totally obsessed with pastries? Sure. But did she love being a pastry chef? No way. I kept thinking that she was going to end up having high blood pressure or maybe even a heart attack. She was always so wound up."

Beatrice said, "It sounds like she was a real perfectionist."

Liam gave a short laugh. "That's a polite way of putting it. Yeah, she was a perfectionist."

"I know you said you didn't know Arabella well, but what were your impressions of her?"

Liam said, "I wasn't crazy about her, either. She was like Nadia—she had really high expectations of me. I didn't mind, really, because I was there to push myself and to learn. The problem was, she thought I should work all the time for just peanuts. For something like that huge party, Arabella should have given me a tip or a bonus or something. But she didn't do it. I worked myself to death for hours for nothing but experience."

"And Arabella expected nothing less?"

"Right. She thought she was giving me a tremendous opportunity, and that I should be endlessly grateful for the exposure." He shook his head. "But this wasn't enough for me to want to murder Arabella. See what I'm saying?"

Beatrice asked, "Why do the police think you might have?"

"They think Arabella knew or had evidence that I'd killed Nadia, and I had to shut her up. Nothing could be farther from the truth. I was just planning on leaving Dappled Hills when this gig was over and never working for her again. At least not for a private party. I wouldn't mind working at one of her events."

Beatrice said, "It might help if you could point the police to somebody else. Just to get them off your back. Now that you've had time to think, is there someone who might have been upset with Arabella? Enough to want to murder her?"

He frowned. "There's a woman who kept calling Arabella all the time. Arabella even mentioned she'd shown up at the house a few times."

"Here in Dappled Hills?" asked Beatrice.

"That's right. Arabella was very frustrated about it." Liam gave a short laugh. "Actually, frustrated isn't the right word. Furious is a better one. The woman was being really obnoxious. I overheard Arabella telling the housekeeper about it. She told Betty she shouldn't let that woman in under any circumstances."

"Sounds like that might have been scary for Arabella."

Liam said, "I'm not sure she was scared, but she was determined not to have to interact with the woman. Whoever she was. Apparently, she and Arabella went way back. Arabella was talking about getting a restraining order on her. Who knows—maybe she's the one who killed her."

"Did you tell the police about this woman?"

"Sure. But they didn't act like they thought it was important." Liam scoffed. "The woman told Arabella 'I could kill you!' one time when she showed up at the door. The cops are passing over a prime suspect."

Beatrice was pretty sure the woman was Emily, who'd lost her boyfriend to Arabella years ago.

Liam said, "She's not the only one who was upset with Arabella, either. Betty, the housekeeper? She couldn't stand her. She was real bitter that she'd raised Arabella's son and wasn't even treated like a member of the family. Betty had never even gotten a raise during all those years she had worked for Arabella."

Liam shook his head angrily. "The more I talk about it, the more I realize there were *lots* more people with a real motive to kill Arabella than me. It just would work out really well for the cops if I were the one who did it, because I'm an outsider. Whenever I go out in town, I feel like people here are staring at me because they know I'm not from around here."

Beatrice frowned. "Really? I think of Dappled Hills as a pretty welcoming town. And we're used to tourists here, especially this time of year. There are lots of folks coming in to shop or experience Christmas in the mountains."

But Liam didn't seem to have heard her. He continued, "Small towns are all alike, aren't they? Everyone keeps to themselves. Which is fine, since I'm going to leave this town as soon as the cops tell me it's okay." Quickly changing the subject, he said, "What did you think of the funeral yesterday?"

"It was lovely," said Beatrice politely. There had been aspects of the funeral that she'd heard people say were over-the-top, but she didn't mention that.

Liam nodded. "It went pretty well, considering it had to be thrown together so fast. I mean, there were some things Oscar was thinking about doing that I thought were gaudy. I'm glad he ended up kicking those ideas to the curb. When he called me up, I was hoping he wasn't going to go through with the stuff. He was talking about an ice sculpture of Arabella and a cake that was a bust of her." He shook his head. "Yeah. Sometimes people just have too much money and not enough sense. Anyway, I was just glad to get some money coming in, like I was telling you yesterday." He looked around him morosely. "What do people do around here?"

Beatrice frowned. "Well, they go to community events like this one. Then there are church and school activities. They go hiking. I'm part of a quilt guild and it seems like there's always something going on with that group."

She could tell Liam wasn't very impressed with the activities Dappled Hills had to offer. She also felt like there was something off. Was he lying to her? He had seemed sort of shifty to her since she had met him.

Liam had apparently decided his conversation with Beatrice needed to draw to a close. "Good talking to you," he said pointedly. "I better go. I want to grab something to eat."

Chapter Seventeen

It was good timing because Wyatt hurried up to join her. "Hey, I didn't realize, but there's a booth for pets here. They can have their picture taken with Santa Paws."

Beatrice was a little distracted, still thinking about Liam. "Hmm."

Wyatt quirked his eyebrow. "Do you think I should go get Noo-noo? That might make for a cute picture."

"What?"

Wyatt looked at her more closely. "Everything okay?"

"I'm sorry—my brain was a million miles away. You said something about Noo-noo?"

Wyatt nodded. "They have a photo booth for pets. Santa Paws."

"Aww. That sounds really cute." She paused. "But it'll be a hassle to go home and grab Noo-noo, won't it?"

Wyatt grinned. "It's not like I'm doing anything else especially important. We're just here to enjoy ourselves. I don't think it'll take me that long. I can also drop off our puddings in the fridge at home so we can eat them whenever. And Noo-noo would have a blast, seeing all the different people at the craft fair."

"Let's do it," said Beatrice. "We could use a cute picture of Noo-noo. I could put it on the fridge along with Will's masterpieces."

So Wyatt dashed off to the parking lot. Beatrice hoped he'd be able to find a parking spot when he came back. She walked on to Posy and Cork's booth. Cork's wine shop had a wine tasting, she remembered. And she believed there might also be eggnog there.

Posy's face lit up when she joined them. Cork gave her a quick greeting. He always came off as a bit cranky, but when you got to know him, you realized he simply had a taciturn nature. He was doling out eggnog to customers on the other side of the bar.

"Oh, glad you're here, Beatrice. It's good to see you. In a slightly better circumstance than a funeral reception, especially."

Beatrice said, "Although it was a very nice reception. I think Arabella's business partner was right. It's exactly what Arabella would have wanted. I'm sure she wouldn't have changed a thing."

A couple came in for a wine tasting. "Do you need help?" Posy asked Cork. He shook his head. The eggnog people had left, so he'd been freed up.

Posy said in a low voice, "I was going to ask you what you thought was going on. Have you learned anything from Ramsay?" She flushed a little. "It's just that some of Cork's and my customers were worrying about safety in downtown Dappled Hills. Although business has still been brisk, I've been wondering if maybe it would be better if someone was arrested. Right now, people are saying Arabella was mugged downtown."

Beatrice shook her head firmly. "I can't imagine that was a random act of violence. I've been wondering if Arabella was the intended target the first time around."

Posy's eyes grew large. "You mean at the party? You think somebody got confused and killed Nadia instead of Arabella?" She frowned. "But Nadia didn't look at all like Arabella, did she?"

"No, she didn't. But maybe Nadia was aware of a plot to murder Arabella. Then she was murdered because she knew too much."

"Ohh," said Posy slowly. "How awful. Poor Nadia. And I feel terrible for Arabella, too. All those years of hard work and then she's killed in the prime of her life. It's an awful thing. I hope Ramsay is about to find out who did it." She leaned in a little closer. "Who are the suspects? Not June Bug, I hope. I heard she was also near the scene of Arabella's death. Surely Ramsay wouldn't think she has anything to do with it?"

"I don't think so. June Bug was just at the wrong place at the wrong time for both deaths. Plus, she didn't really have a reason to murder Nadia or Arabella. She wasn't around them all that much—just for the party. Besides, there are plenty of other people who have better reasons to be angry with Arabella."

Posy looked relieved. "Oh, that's good. I've been worried about poor June Bug. I keep feeling like she does so much for others, and she really doesn't have anyone to take care of *her*."

Just then, a group of customers came into the booth. "I'd better run," said Posy reluctantly. "Maybe I'll see you around the craft fair later."

Beatrice visited more of the crafts. She especially marveled over the pottery and glassware displayed in a couple of nearby booths. Some of the pottery was practical as well as beautiful, in the form of bowls, mugs, plates, and platters in earthy tones of forest green, deep brown, and stone gray. Some of the pottery was meant to be purely decorative, with vases and sculptures as statement pieces. The glassware booth displayed some fused glass that was particularly beautiful, as the artist had layered and melted different pieces of glass to create unique jewelry and art panels.

Wyatt texted her to let her know he'd found a parking spot and that he and Noo-noo would meet her at the Santa Paws booth. Beatrice looked at the map online and headed over to the booth.

Apparently, Wyatt and Noo-noo had been stopped quite a few times along the way. Wyatt, as the minister, was often a draw, but with Noo-noo, Beatrice imagined that they'd have people trying to greet them even more. She looked around the Santa Paws booth while she waited for Wyatt to show up. It was decked out with a red and green striped canopy and garlands strewn with twinkling lights. A plush throne was at the center where a very authentic Santa welcomed each furry customer. A backdrop behind the throne featured a snow-covered landscape, reindeer, and a sleigh. Beatrice noticed there was a basket full of pet-friendly treats and toys in case any of the animals needed extra enticement. There was also a small area to the side that had festive pet costumes and accessories, ranging from reindeer antlers to elf hats.

She got another text from Wyatt, apologizing and saying they were making slow progress across the fairground.

Beatrice heard a voice behind her and turned to see Melissa Martin—the woman whose husband had been having the affair with Nadia. "Hi there," said Beatrice. She looked down at the tiny dog Melissa was holding and said, "And hi to you!"

Melissa looked pleased at the attention her furbaby was getting. "Isn't she adorable? Her name is Bella."

Bella was a Chihuahua, no larger than a teacup. She seemed to be very well taken care of. Her coat was a glossy chestnut, and she wore a tiny red sweater with a green Christmas tree knitted on the back. Bella's big, round eyes seemed to hold a mix of excitement and apprehension as she surveyed the large bearded man on the throne. Beatrice figured it was probably a good thing that there were a couple of other dogs in line first. That would give Bella the opportunity to settle down before it was her turn.

"How are things going?" asked Beatrice cautiously. Melissa had certainly not been shy about her fury over her husband's affair the last time they spoke.

"Oh, everything's okay. At first, I felt sort of embarrassed going out in public, but I've decided that's ridiculous. *I* haven't done anything wrong."

Beatrice said, "You certainly haven't. I'm glad you're getting out of the house."

"Exactly. I know people are probably talking, but let them talk."

Beatrice said, "They probably don't know anything about what happened. I haven't heard any gossip."

Melissa gave her a rueful look. "Well, maybe they're trying not to gossip with the minister's wife. The truth is, I decided I'm not taking Hal back." She sniffed. "Let him be someone else's problem. They can have him and all his nonsense, if he's so determined to see other people."

"Is Hal seeing someone now?" asked Beatrice. She was slightly shocked at the idea. It seemed to be a lot—cheating on your wife, then losing the woman you were having an affair with. Taking on someone else seemed extreme.

"Who knows?" said Melissa in a determinedly cheerful tone. "It's not any of my business now. I've secured a lawyer and am making sure he will be officially out of my life soon." She leaned in close to Beatrice. "I heard you were the one to find Arabella. That must have been awful."

"It was," said Beatrice honestly. "I'd just spoken to her a few minutes before, and it was hard to believe she was gone."

"Well, no matter what the cops believe, I had nothing to do with Arabella's death." Melissa pressed her lips together in annoyance at the thought they might suspect her.

"Have they been asking you questions?"

"It feels like they've been hounding me, actually," said Melissa. "Or they *were*. Until I gave them a completely rock-solid alibi for Arabella's death. I was at work—at the post office. I have lots of witnesses and the police are totally satisfied that I had nothing to do with it."

Beatrice said, "Oh, I bet this time of year, you probably *do* have to work Sundays."

"At Christmas? Yeah. There's a huge amount of mail volume. Plus, we do have packages to deliver on Sundays. Naturally, they're short-staffed, so they called me to come in. At first, I was really irritated about it. But now I'm glad I had to go into work. Otherwise, the cops would be trying to pin Arabella's death on me, too."

Bella gave her owner a glum look, most likely because of the Christmas sweater she was reluctantly wearing. But the timing made it look like she was commiserating with Melissa for being a suspect.

"Anyway, if you could help spread the word that I have an alibi for Arabella's death, that would be awesome. I feel like everybody is talking about me right now, and I want it to stop. But I'm not going to hide at home, like I told you."

Beatrice gave her a sympathetic look. "I'm sorry you've had to go through all this. And right before Christmas, too."

Melissa shrugged. "Thanks. I felt pretty sorry for myself at first, but now I'm coming to terms with it all. I'd rather know Hal is a cheater than find out later he'd been with several women." She gave Beatrice a curious look. "Have you heard anything about Arabella's death? Who might have done it?"

Beatrice turned the question around on her. "Who do *you* think might have done it?"

Melissa considered this. "I'm thinking Arabella's maid. Or housekeeper, whatever. When I was trying to gather up my courage to approach Nadia at the Christmas party, I overheard the way Arabella was talking to Betty. She was unbelievably rude. I mean, it was really inexcusable. Plus, I saw Betty acting suspiciously at the party. Kind of sneaking around . . . staying in the shadows."

Beatrice wondered if Betty were simply acting that way because she wanted to avoid another encounter with Arabella. It seemed like she'd have wanted to take a breather if Arabella had been on top of her all the time.

Melissa sighed. "I'm sure plenty of people still think I had something to do with Nadia's death. I get it—I had a good motive. But they shouldn't think that way. Yes, I was going to tell Nadia off in a public place. My goal was to make her feel rotten for being a home-wrecker. But I had absolutely no plans to do anything else." Suddenly, she froze. "I can't believe it. He's here."

Beatrice turned to look. She was relieved to see Hal was by himself, not with a date. He had dark hair and was lean and fit, but had a drawn face and exhausted eyes. He paused when he saw Melissa clutching Bella. Bella gave a light growl, whether to warn Melissa she was holding her too closely or whether to scare off Melissa's husband, Beatrice wasn't sure.

He approached, holding his hands in front of him beseechingly.

Melissa said in a curt voice, "Look, I'm here having a good time. We have nothing to talk about."

Hal gave Beatrice a slight, apologetic smile. "Just a second. I just wanted to talk to you for a second."

Melissa heaved a big sigh. "Okay. You've got a second. It's almost Bella's turn with Santa."

He nodded, as if he understood. Then he said, "I just wanted to ask for your forgiveness. I know what I did was incredibly wrong. Like I told you, I've never done anything like that before."

"It doesn't matter. You've done it now." Melissa's eyes narrowed.

Hal said in a rush, "You're right. I'm just as guilty as if I'd been unfaithful multiple times." He was quiet for a moment. "Maybe asking for your forgiveness is too much of an ask. Scratch that—it would be really too generous for you to overlook something like that. What I really want is for us to at least part as friends. We had lots of good years and good times together, didn't we?"

Melissa gave a small, reluctant nod. "I'm not taking you back, you know."

He hung his head. "Yes, I know that. I screwed all that up. But I'd really like us to move forward as friends."

Melissa considered this for a minute. "That's almost like asking for forgiveness. It's not something I can do right away." She paused. "I'll keep trying to think of you as a friend. I'll try."

Hal looked relieved. "Thanks, Melissa." He reached out to give her a quick hug, but Bella snarled at him, and he jerked back. "Uh, see you around town." He hurried away.

Melissa gave a short laugh. "Well, that was a surprise," she said slowly.

"Will it make things less-stressful? Embarking on a friendship with your ex?"

Melissa was quiet for a moment. "You know, I think it might. You just never know. It's not something that's going to happen overnight, though. I'm a little too bitter right now."

The photographer called for Bella, and Melissa grinned. "Here we go!"

The session took a few minutes longer because Bella was in a very cranky mood following the appearance of Melissa's husband. The tiny chihuahua was giving the photographer quite a baleful look, as well as Santa, who she was especially suspicious about. Santa cheered her up a bit with treats, but she was still gazing at him through narrowed eyes. Finally, Melissa got in front of Bella, cooing at her, which made her face light up for some good pictures.

Wyatt and Noo-noo walked into the booth. Wyatt gave Beatrice an apologetic look. "Sorry that took so long. I think I must have run into every single person I know." He looked down affectionately at the corgi. "And Noo-noo didn't help much, either. She was grinning at everyone."

Noo-noo, unlike Bella the chihuahua, was indeed in an excellent mood. She was turning her foxlike grin at Beatrice now, with the desired results, as Beatrice stooped to give the dog a cuddle. Noo-noo watched with interest as Bella ended up her photo session with Santa, and Melissa walked over with an elf to discuss which photos she wanted.

"You're up," said the photographer cheerfully to them. Santa gave a hearty ho-ho-ho, which Noo-noo loved, then hoisted the corgi up on his generous lap. He proceeded to chat with Noo-noo while the photographer snapped pictures.

"I can't wait to see these," said Wyatt, laughing. "Noo-noo seems to be having a hard time sitting still. I guess she's still so excited about being at the craft fair."

When Wyatt and Beatrice followed the elf to see the results, they burst into laughter. One photo showed Noo-noo with a huge, tongue-out smile and bright eyes that sparkled with mischief as she stared at Santa's beard.

"It looks like she's trying to decide if his beard is real," said Beatrice.

"It's one-hundred percent genuine," the elf said with a big smile.

The next picture showed Noo-noo looking at Santa with a curious expression, head tilted to one side, her large eyes perplexed.

But the next was their favorite. As Noo-noo got more comfortable sitting in Santa's lap, she nuzzled against him, looking contented.

"That's the one," said Beatrice.

The elf gave Noo-noo a treat for a job well done. "I think yours is the easiest dog we've had today," said the elf.

"Good job, Noo-noo!" said Wyatt.

And the three of them walked out to enjoy the rest of their evening at the craft fair.

Chapter Eighteen

The next morning, Beatrice slept in a bit. Fortunately, Wyatt and Noo-noo both did, too. They'd spent longer at the craft fair than they'd originally thought they would. They met up with Will, who was very excited to see Noo-noo in a different setting than he ordinarily did. Meadow had been relieved from booth duty by Savannah and Georgia and delightedly escorted Will and Piper around the fair. It was fun to see everything through Will's eyes because everything was new and surprising.

But all the excitement meant Beatrice had a tough time falling asleep that night. Thus the late start the next morning. Beatrice also noticed that, although she'd run plenty of Christmas-related errands lately, she hadn't been to the grocery store. Nor, apparently, had Wyatt because the refrigerator had not a trace of an egg or cheese or milk.

"I can run to the store for you," said Wyatt, still rubbing sleep from his eyes as he reached for the coffeemaker.

"No, I'll go. Tomorrow is Christmas Eve, which is one of your busiest days of the year. Besides, I'm not sure what I need to buy. I'll make a short list of things I *know* we're out of, or almost out of. That was the last of the coffee, for one thing."

Wyatt raised his eyebrows. "Now *that* is an emergency."

"Exactly."

Beatrice got ready, jotted out a list, and drove off for Bub's grocery. It was an old-fashioned grocery store that had been around for ages. There were three wooden rocking chairs in front of the store with three old men who hung out there every day. They were such fixtures that everyone would put out missing posters if they weren't there one day.

Beatrice got a cart and peered at her list. Coffee, milk, eggs. Did they even have bread? She decided if anything was in question, she should just get it. The store would be closed for Christmas for the next two days, and she didn't want to run out of anything.

Beatrice was studying the vegetables in the produce section when she spotted Emily Nash doing the same thing. Beatrice cleared her throat. "Hi, Emily. Merry Christmas."

Emily had been deep in thought and started when she heard Beatrice call her name. "Oh, Beatrice. Merry Christmas to you, too."

"How is everything going?" Beatrice thought again about Emily's anger against Arabella. Had things gotten better with Arabella gone? Or was that long-time bitterness still there because Arabella had stolen her high school boyfriend? It had been such a powerful emotion Emily felt that it seemed unlikely to disappear just because Arabella had died.

Initially, it appeared that Emily didn't really want to discuss the murders. "Oh, it's going okay. Like you, I figured I better get to the store before it closed for the holidays. Although I'm having a tough time remembering what I need." She snapped her fingers. "I was also going to look up to see what times the Christmas Eve services are. I'm guessing you know."

Beatrice recited them off by heart. The times never changed, but people had a tough time remembering when the children's service, the adult service, and the midnight-ending candlelight service took place. Although she supposed the candlelight service was easier to recall.

"Okay, good," said Emily. "I'll be sure to be there." She paused, then reluctantly asked, "I always hate talking about this, because it puts me in such a weird mood. But do you have any updates on the murders? I know you see Meadow and Ramsay a lot."

"I don't have updates, no. I understand that the police are talking to everyone and trying to narrow down possibilities." It was a very vague statement, but Beatrice didn't want to give anything away.

Emily nodded unhappily. "Yeah, I know about them talking to people. They've been pestering me, too. They're totally convinced my bad blood with Arabella meant I took revenge on her."

"After all these years?"

Emily made a face. "The cops apparently think revenge is a dish best served cold." Beatrice saw tears spring to her eyes, and Emily hastily blinked them away. "I know I should have gotten over Pete by now. I've been stuck in the past and haven't been able to move forward. But you know, I'd pictured the future so perfectly with him. When I lost Pete, it's like my life took a completely different trajectory. A much harder one."

Beatrice said in a gentle voice, "It sounds like you've been grieving, Emily. It's not just that you lost a boyfriend. You lost the future you'd envisioned. And grief is hard to move past. Everyone's experience with grief is different." She paused. "Maybe you should talk things out with somebody. A licensed therapist. Or Wyatt, if you feel comfortable doing that. He has a way of helping people figure life out."

"Thanks, Beatrice," said Emily, tearing up again. "You're right. I've got to find a way to put the past behind me—for my sake."

Beatrice spontaneously reached out and gave her a hug. "You've been through a tough time."

Emily nodded. She hesitated. "I've been thinking a lot about who might have committed these crimes. It was an awful thing to happen to both those women. Arabella didn't deserve what happened to her. I know I . . . didn't like her. But that didn't mean I wished her harm. Now *she's* lost the bright future that was ahead of her, too."

"Have you come up with anyone who might be a suspect?"

Emily looked around cautiously to make sure no one was listening in. She said, "I know I was talking about Ruth when Ramsay asked me that question. But she's just such a sweet person. I can't see her murdering her sister, no matter how Arabella treated her. I was wondering if maybe that assistant pastry chef guy had an affair with Arabella."

Beatrice frowned. "Liam? Have you heard any rumors?"

Emily shook her head. "No, nothing like that. I didn't even know his name, but I've seen him around town. It would have been just like Arabella to have a dalliance with somebody that young. Maybe she dumped him afterward like she dumped Pete. Maybe Liam got angry about her attitude and shoved her down the stairs."

It was a lot of conjecture. Beatrice said, "Well, it sounds like a possibility. Maybe that's the way it happened."

Emily flushed, glancing at her watch. "I'm sorry to have taken up so much of your time. I know how busy you must be right before Christmas. And thanks for telling me about Wyatt. I might go have a talk with him sometime after the new year."

With that, she hurried away, leaving Beatrice to look blankly at the vegetables again as she tried to process all the thoughts running through her mind. She had the terrible feeling this might be a day where she had to return to the grocery store to pick up all the bits and pieces she'd forgotten.

Beatrice made it all the way to the paper products aisle and was proud she remembered they were out of paper towels. The store had gotten even more crowded during her conversation with Emily. She turned the corner to the next aisle and saw Georgia standing there.

Georgia said, "Beatrice! Merry Christmas. I didn't get to see you at the craft fair."

Beatrice winced. "Oops. Wyatt and I meant to go back to the booth after you relieved Meadow. We met up with Piper and Will and didn't make it back over there."

"Oh, no worries! I know how it goes. Things get busy, don't they?"

Beatrice chuckled. "That's right—you've been on costume duty for the Christmas play. How did all that go?"

"It was just fine. Easy-peasy, actually, and a nice way to help out. I wouldn't have wanted Edgenora's job, though."

"Heavens, no!" said Beatrice. "I should have checked in on her again before now. I know she was under a ton of stress the last time I saw her. Mostly because of casting, at the time."

They chatted for a few minutes, catching up. Then Georgia said, "I saw Emily leaving the store when I was coming in. Do you know her?"

"I'm just barely acquainted, although we talked for a few minutes over in the produce department."

Georgia said, "Oh good, I'm glad you were talking to her. I've gotten the impression that she's been having a hard time recently. Actually, she's been having a *really* hard time since she was in high school. We're neighbors, so I've been able to get to know her."

"It seems like she's had a tough time reinventing her life after losing Pete. She's stuck, and I don't think she wants to be stuck anymore."

"Exactly," said Georgia. "She's frustrated with where she is, but can't seem to move forward. I've tried to help her see the big picture, that she has friends and people who care about her, but it just doesn't work."

Beatrice said, "Bitterness can be so corrosive. That's really hard."

"I had hopes when she'd told me she'd gotten an invitation to Arabella's party and was planning on attending. I thought maybe that would be the way to finally put the past behind her."

Beatrice's eyes were wide. "But Emily wasn't at the party. She said she wasn't invited."

Georgia looked confused. "Maybe you just missed her. Emily told me she didn't stay long, but she was proud of herself for going." She glanced at her watch. "Ugh, I better finish with my shopping. I've got to run by Savannah's after this and pick up the costumes for the play. Good talking to you, Beatrice."

After Beatrice returned home and put the groceries away, she sat on the sofa, petting Noo-noo, who snuggled up with her. The little dog could probably tell her mind was spinning with everything swirling through it. Emily had been at Arabella's party. But that didn't mean Emily had killed Nadia and Arabella. She might have just, understandably, wanted to distance herself from a crime scene. When Emily told Georgia she'd been at the party, she probably hadn't yet heard that a murder had taken place there. After all, Georgia said she was only there for a short time.

But why would Emily have murdered Nadia? If she was going off the assumption that Nadia was killed because she was aware of a plot to murder Arabella, then how would she have found out Emily's plans?

Maybe they were all wrong, and Nadia was killed not because she knew something, but because of a personal reason. Perhaps Arabella was murdered in a completely separate incident. If that was the case, Melissa Martin had the best motive to eliminate Nadia. Her husband was having an affair with her. No one else seemed to have a direct motive to kill Nadia.

Except for Liam. Nadia had been a tough taskmaster, and Liam was determined to make it as a pastry chef and seemed to have a lot of talent. What if Nadia had decided to give Liam a bad recommendation? Coming from a star in the field like Nadia, it could have had devastating repercussions for his career.

In terms of Arabella's death, there were a few people who had clear motives. Betty Boxer, her loyal housekeeper, had put years of hard work in caring for Arabella's different homes—and even Arabella's son, Bruce, whom she'd helped to raise. From all accounts, Arabella was either dismissive of Betty or treated her as if she were invisible. Over the years, could Betty have gotten progressively more angry and frustrated?

Ruth Chamberlain was another possibility. Arabella appeared to have left her with the tough caregiving work with their mother. Then, when Ruth hadn't been able to hold down a job because of her need to care for their mom, Arabella hadn't helped Ruth out financially when asked. This was another instance where her anger could have been something that built up over time. Maybe it just released when she started seeing Arabella frequently after she returned to Dappled Hills.

Then Oscar Baldwin came to mind. He'd helped Arabella build their event business into a tremendous success and had worked on the accounting and human resources end, which Arabella apparently hadn't been as interested in. He'd been in town earlier than he'd claimed and seemed like he was carefully holding information back. Arabella had told Beatrice she planned on dissolving their partnership. Had Oscar gotten wind of this plan? Did he decide to murder Arabella and take over the business?

Beatrice sighed and Noo-noo looked up at her with concern. Stewing over the suspects didn't seem to do any good.

Maybe she needed to get out of the house. It was lunchtime, and she suddenly decided it would be good to enjoy lunch with Wyatt. Considering it was December 23rd, and on the late end of lunch, she texted him to make sure he hadn't already eaten and that he wasn't extremely busy. Learning he was open, she made a couple of sandwiches, grabbed some red grapes and two cookies, and headed out of the house.

The church parking lot was busy, and it occurred to Beatrice that it must be time for the dress rehearsal for the Christmas play. She decided to stick her head in after eating lunch with Wyatt. Beatrice especially wanted to see how Edgenora was coping with being the play's director. Hopefully, things were going better than they'd started out.

Wyatt was typing away at his computer, reading glasses on. He smiled when Beatrice walked in. "Thanks for suggesting lunch. Today has been so busy that I might have totally forgotten about it if you hadn't texted me."

"Now *that* would have been bad. I seem to remember you usually get headaches when you don't eat regularly."

"Sadly true," admitted Wyatt. "Thanks for saving me from that fate."

Beatrice unpacked the sandwiches, fruit, and cookies, and they chatted for a few minutes. Beatrice mentioned her trip to the store and talking with Emily and Georgia. Wyatt said that he'd been visiting elderly and disabled members of the congregation to make sure they had contact with the church before Christmas.

Wyatt said, "Have we worked out the logistics for Christmas?"

"I think so. Meadow and Ramsay invited us to come over to their place for Christmas brunch and exchanging presents."

Wyatt grinned. "That sounds like a delicious proposition. I know Meadow's brunches are pretty extraordinary."

"Yes, I think she could even put Arabella's events to shame. She's talking about making her famous country ham biscuits and her cheesy grits casserole. Oh, and some pecan pie muffins."

Wyatt said, "How can my stomach be growling when I'm already halfway through eating my lunch?"

"Because you know how delectable Meadow's down-home cooking is."

Wyatt munched on his sandwich for a moment before asking, "Are you and I exchanging gifts before we go over to the Downeys' house?"

"Definitely. Otherwise, our presents for each other might get lost in the wrapping paper of the gift exchange over there."

Wyatt and Beatrice had decided before Thanksgiving to just have simple presents for each other that year. They weren't cutting back on gift giving for anyone else, but wanted to have a simpler Christmas and focus on the joy of being with family and each other.

"How does your afternoon look?" Beatrice took another bite of her chicken salad sandwich.

"Busy," said Wyatt wryly. "For some reason, the session decided we should start in with budget reviews and planning for next year now. Usually, we do it the week after Christmas."

Beatrice made a face. "That's a little crazy to squeeze it in now, isn't it? Right before the holidays?"

"I think somebody mentioned a couple of members of the session are going to be out of town visiting family. It's fine, it just means a few more meetings than I'd planned for. But I've got the Christmas Eve services nailed down, so at least that's finished."

After they finished eating, Wyatt said reluctantly, "I guess I'd better get back to it. Thanks so much for coming over. I think I needed a midday break."

"Try not to overdo things too much. I'll see you later. I'm going to check in on the Christmas play rehearsals and see how things are going for Edgenora."

"Good idea," said Wyatt. "She's worth her weight in gold. I hope *she* hasn't been overdoing things too much."

Beatrice gave him a kiss goodbye, then headed off for the family life center, where the play rehearsals were being held.

Chapter Nineteen

On the way to check in with Edgenora, Beatrice saw Betty Boxer mopping the hallway. She smiled when she saw Beatrice. "Hi there," said Betty.

"Merry Christmas to you! It looks like you've gotten the custodial job at the church."

Betty smiled at her. She looked a lot more energized and less tired and worried than the last time Beatrice had spoken with her.

"That's right. They were able to give me full-time hours, too, which is wonderful."

Beatrice said, "I'm so glad that worked out. And I know the church admin is going to be delighted with your work." It was clear Betty was not only experienced, she was a hard worker. She wondered if the church pay was in any way equivalent to what she'd been making as Arabella's housekeeper. Beatrice guessed it wasn't, but on the other hand, Betty wasn't having to deal with Arabella's behavior.

A hint of the worry Beatrice had seen last time sneaked its way back into her features. "Thanks. I hope it all works out. I'm a little worried about what the police are thinking about Nadia and Arabella's deaths. If they get really serious about me being a suspect, I might not be able to keep this job."

"I'm sure everything will work out fine. The police are just going through their usual protocol."

Betty nodded, but her expression was still pinched. She said hesitantly, "Someone told the police that they'd witnessed Arabella and me arguing. I was so taken by surprise when the cops mentioned it, I wasn't prepared. I hope I didn't make matters worse."

"Did you tell the police what Arabella was really like? What your life with her was like?"

Betty sighed. "I didn't want to. To me, that made it sound like I had even more motive to want Arabella gone. But I did finally tell them because I wanted to explain why we'd been arguing." She leaned against the mop. "I was mostly speaking from a place of hurt. I'd bitten my tongue for so many years."

"I understand that you'd helped raise Arabella's son, Bruce."

Betty looked proud. "That's right. And he's a fine, young man. Arabella was often traveling for work, and needed someone to keep an eye on Bruce. I tried to do more than that because I could see he was lonely. We spent a lot of time together, the two of us. But Arabella never acknowledged my help." Betty shook her head. "When I'm saying this, it sounds really petty. And here we are standing in a church right before Christmas."

"It doesn't sound petty at all. It sounds like you felt hurt."

Betty said, "You're right. I was hurt. Arabella never really spoke to me unless she was asking me to do something. Or to *redo* something that I'd already done. Everything had to be spotless all the time and everything had to be to her specifications.

I understood that, because she was the boss. But wanting all the labels to be facing the same direction in the pantry, especially when she never cooked, felt like a little much."

"She really did that? Wow. She'd hate the way my cabinets look right now. I went to the grocery store earlier today and just shoved everything in wherever I could find a spot." Beatrice paused. "You were in charge of actually doing most of the shopping, too, right? I think I remember your saying that."

"Exactly. I did grocery shopping, picked up the dry cleaning, and ran any other errands that were required by the household."

Beatrice said, "Those seem more like things a personal assistant would handle than a housekeeper. I mean, you had a huge job already. That house was massive, and I understand that wasn't Arabella's only dwelling."

"That's right. She also had a home in Palm Springs and a place in Aspen."

Beatrice said, "And you handled it all yourself. It seems like you should have had staff of your own to manage, just like the housekeepers in the old days used to—like *Downton Abbey*."

"Well, that would have made life easier, for sure," said Betty with a laugh. "But that's not the way it worked out. Anyway, the long-winded point I'm making is that I filled the police in on the scope of the work I was doing, the hours I was putting in, and the lack of recognition, or really even basic civility I was getting from Arabella. Was it professional for me to blow my top? No. Did I do it? Yes."

"What was Arabella's reaction when you finally told her off?"

Betty smiled a little. "She was stunned. Genuinely stunned. I'd always done precisely what Arabella had wanted me to without questioning her. I guess it was the straw that broke the camel's back when I finally spoke back to her."

"What was the straw?"

"Something silly. Arabella said I hadn't done a good enough job cleaning the crystal chandelier. That it didn't sparkle enough, and I should redo it." Betty shook her head. "Cleaning that thing had already taken hours of work. I should never have said anything, but I did."

"I can certainly understand that," said Beatrice. "I'm sure the fact that you put your relationship with Arabella in context have helped the police to have a clearer picture."

"Let's just hope the clearer picture isn't that I'm the murderer," said Betty with a short laugh.

"I'm sure it's going to be okay. And I'm glad you're here at the church," said Beatrice.

She left Betty to her mopping and walked to the family life center. Beatrice stood at the door, smiling for a few moments. It was a dress rehearsal, so all the little ones were in costume. The youngest children were lambs and other animals. Edgenora was having an earnest discussion with little Joseph, explaining where he needed to stand. The shepherds were chasing each other around the gym. The angels sat in a circle, like the little angels they were dressed as, and having a conversation. One of the lambs had fallen asleep in a pile on the floor, chubby arms under his head.

The parents seemed to be everywhere, some waiting to talk to Edgenora, some trying to pin the costumes so they fit their child a bit better. One was giving her child a snack of what appeared to be pretzels and other children were flocking around him, hoping to get some themselves.

Beatrice glanced at her watch. They were coming to the top of the hour, and she assumed

the dress rehearsal must be nearly over. The kids' energy was flagging, aside from the shepherds', and it would be like herding cats if the practice went on much longer.

Sure enough, Edgenora raised her voice to get everyone's attention, thanking them for coming to practice, and reminding them when they needed to show up for the play the next day. Then she walked over to see Beatrice.

"How did the dress rehearsal go?" asked Beatrice.

Edgenora smiled. "It was hilarious on the one hand and productive on the other. It's tough to keep everyone's attention focused at this age, so we just do the best we can."

"That's exactly the right attitude. Nobody's coming to the children's service tomorrow expecting to see a Broadway production. And sometimes, when the kids mess up, it makes the whole thing even more adorable and memorable."

"Now that's the right way to think about it," said Edgenora slowly. "Thanks, Beatrice. Sometimes I'm too much of a perfectionist."

"Well, that works really well for you as a church administrator. And we like you just the way you are." Beatrice paused. "Hey, I ran into Betty Boxer on the way over here. How is she working out?"

Edgenora beamed. "Like a dream. She's a fellow perfectionist, I believe. Betty is totally on top of everything."

"I'm glad to hear it. I know she needed a job, and I'm happy she's working out so well."

Edgenora said, "Betty is more than just working out. She gets into every nook and cranny. I've spotted her moving furniture to clean behind and underneath it. And she's been working on ceiling air vents and light fixtures. She's like a machine."

The two women chatted for a few more minutes before Edgenora said, "Well, I guess I better head out. Tomorrow's a big day, and I should rest up for it." Then she made an irritated face. "Ugh. I need to run by the store to grab batteries first, though. One of the cordless microphones is out of them."

"I can do that for you. What kind of batteries are they?"

Edgenora hesitated. "I hate to ask you to do that. It's not like you're not busy, yourself."

"No, it's my pleasure."

"They're AA batteries. That would be really helpful, if you don't mind. You could just bring them to the service a few minutes early tomorrow."

Beatrice said, "No problem. I'll come about twenty minutes early so you can do a sound check."

Shortly, Beatrice was leaving the still-crowded church parking lot and heading to the store for the batteries. Directly next to the store was a historic hotel in downtown Dappled Hills. Oscar Baldwin was in the parking lot, quickly placing bags in the trunk of a car. And suddenly, it jogged Beatrice's memory. She remembered what she'd found confusing during her recent conversation with Liam.

She called out to Oscar, and he turned swiftly, giving a tight bob of his head.

"Heading back home?" she asked.

"Yes, I think it's time. Of course, I was glad to be here to pull Arabella's funeral together, but I had to put lots of things on hold while I was here." His words were rushed, as if he was ready to leave town. But Beatrice wasn't quite ready to let him go yet.

"It was a lovely service and reception," she said. "Arabella would have thought it was perfect. I can't believe what you were able to pull together in such a short period of time. It was a real testament to your event planning."

Oscar gave her a small smile. "That's kind of you to say. Your husband did a marvelous job with the homily."

"I understand from Liam that you got him on board to help out," said Beatrice in an innocent tone. "And that you'd originally planned even *more* things for the reception. I think Liam mentioned an ice sculpture."

Oscar narrowed his eyes. "Well, we had to forgo some things that I'd have liked to have had at the reception. It was simply a matter of time."

"Understandable. I'm glad you were able to pull it all together so successfully. I hadn't realized you and Liam were in touch. I thought you'd said you hadn't spoken to him."

Oscar was quiet for a moment. "I spoke to Betty, the housekeeper. She made the arrangements."

Which wasn't at all what Liam had said, of course. Beatrice said, "Liam seems to be looking for his next placement, since Nadia isn't around to mentor him right now. It's great that Liam might be able to help you out with future events."

"Yes, he's quite a good pastry chef. He definitely has the makings of a great one." Oscar said quickly, "It was nice to speak with you, but I have to run, I'm afraid. Business calls."

"Of course. Safe travels."

When Beatrice got to the door of the store, she looked back and saw Oscar staring at her.

Beatrice got the batteries and headed back to the cottage, where she let Noo-noo out. Then Wyatt called.

"Hey," he said. "Glad we had lunch together, because it's looking like we won't be spending much time together tonight. Two members of the congregation are in the hospital and doing poorly."

He told Beatrice who they were. "Are they both hospitalized nearby?" asked Beatrice. Dappled Hills had a small hospital, but they sent patients away for services they couldn't provide.

"No, Sally is in Dappled Hills, but George is in Lenoir, so it'll be a drive."

"No problem," said Beatrice. "I'll hold down the fort here."

"Everything going okay? How was Edgenora when you checked on her today?"

"Oh, she was fine. A little stressed out. I reminded her that nobody expects perfection from a preschool and elementary production of a Christmas play."

Wyatt chuckled. "That's the truth. Okay, well, take some time to relax. I'll text you when I'm on my way back home."

Beatrice read her book, *The Christmas Box*, for a few minutes before getting ready to start supper. Since Wyatt was having a long day, she thought she'd make a hot meal for a change. This was the time of year where sometimes they both got so busy that

Beatrice and Wyatt would mostly just make salads for themselves instead of investing time in cooking.

She finished a few chapters, then decided it was time to get started in the kitchen. She decided to make a meatloaf with the things she'd picked up at the store. Noo-noo watched with interest as she combined the ground beef, egg, onion, milk, and bread crumbs. Despite the corgi's fervent wishes, Beatrice managed not to spill anything on the floor. Usually, she didn't enjoy cooking, but felt restless this evening and the process of putting a meal together felt unexpectedly soothing.

Noo-noo whined at the door when she'd popped the meatloaf into the oven. "Need to go out again?" asked Beatrice.

She opened the door to find Liam standing there, holding a gun.

Chapter Twenty

Noo-noo, sensing the tension and having been startled by the unexpected visitor, started barking wildly. "Shut her up," snarled Liam.

Beatrice backed inside the house, then stooped down to put her arms around Noo-noo. "What are you doing?" Beatrice asked, a quaver in her voice.

"What do you think I'm doing?" snapped Liam.

That was a good question. Beatrice decided to take it seriously. She also needed to delay the young man as much as possible. "I think Oscar Baldwin called you up. He told you he thought I knew too much, and that I needed to be eliminated." She looked unsteadily at the gun, carefully standing back up again. "Where'd you get the gun?"

"My dad gave it to me years ago," said Liam with a shrug. "I often take it with me when I travel. Sometimes for protection and sometimes because I can go for target practice if a town has a gun range. Dappled Hills does have one." He aimed it directly at her head, a motion that made Noo-noo growl again.

"The thing is," said Beatrice in as light a tone as she could muster, "I realized Oscar lied to me. He'd said at Arabella's funeral reception that he'd not been in touch with you at all. But it seems, from speaking with you at the craft fair, that he'd called you directly to discuss things like ice sculptures and cakes."

"So?"

"So, Oscar lied. And if Oscar was lying about that, it stands to reason that he could be lying about other things, too. Like murder," said Beatrice.

Liam gave her a sly smile. "Okay, I'd like to hear your deductions. I thought you were just being nosy, but I heard around town that you get involved with police investigations pretty regularly. Like you're a consultant for them or something."

"Nothing official." Beatrice swallowed. She wanted to drag this out as long as possible, even though she knew Wyatt wouldn't be back home for a while. "Deductions, right. This is what I think, knowing what I know now. I think Oscar was the mastermind behind all of this. I don't think this is something you dreamed up."

Liam nodded, the gun still pointed steadily her way.

Beatrice's mouth was feeling very dry now and the corgi at her feet was still making very ominous sounds. She wouldn't be able to stand it if something happened to Noo-noo. Pushing the thought out of her mind, she said, "I believe Oscar wanted to get rid of Arabella all along. Arabella was not the kind of person who hid her feelings. She had very high standards and was something of a control freak. She'd even follow along behind her housekeeper, Betty, to make sure she'd completed chores to her specifications."

"Yeah, so?"

"So Oscar could tell Arabella was thinking twice about their long-term partnership. Maybe he even heard from other people about her plan to dump him as her business partner—Arabella told me she was going to dissolve the partnership, and we didn't even know each other well. Oscar would naturally want to ensure he'd be out of town when Arabella died. He'd want an excellent alibi for her death."

Liam snorted. "Hate to tell you, but Oscar was right here in Dappled Hills when Arabella kicked the bucket." He moved closer toward Beatrice.

"Yes, but that hadn't been the original plan, had it? Oscar wanted you to be his proxy. He wanted you to kill Arabella. Maybe even on the night of her party."

Liam stopped still. "How do you figure that?"

"I think it might have appealed to the showman in Oscar. At any rate, he asked you to murder Arabella for him at a time when he was nowhere close to North Carolina. But something happened, didn't it? Nadia found out the plan. Did she overhear a phone call between you and Oscar?"

Liam didn't answer, just stared at her with cold eyes.

Beatrice took a deep breath and continued. "Oscar must have offered to pay you handsomely for the task. I'm sure the money must have seemed very alluring to you. You're a student still, after all. I'm guessing you might have some loan debt. And it wasn't as if you particularly *liked* Arabella." Her mind was racing. She had to keep Liam talking and buy herself some time.

Liam grunted. "It was Oscar who came up with the whole thing."

"How did Nadia find out about the plan?"

Liam said, "Not sure. The day of Arabella's party, she told me she knew. Maybe she did overhear me on the phone with Oscar. Nadia didn't say."

"Of course, you couldn't let Nadia live after that. It would have been too much of a risk." Beatrice paused. "Did she try to blackmail you about it? Is that why she told you?"

Liam shook his head slowly. "No. Nadia wasn't that kind of person. She told me she was going right to the cops and tell them everything." He gave a short laugh. "She must have been stewing about it because she told me right in the middle of the party. Maybe it made her feel safe, knowing there were so many people in the house."

Beatrice kept listening out for the sound of a car pulling into the driveway, but there was nothing. She took in a shaky breath. "Nadia thought you weren't dangerous. She'd gotten to know you a little during your internship. She probably was also used to being in the role of authority figure with you. But you murdered her, hitting her with the rolling pin, before she had the chance to tell the police what she knew."

Liam said dryly, "It's been a real problem having people know too much."

A shiver went up Beatrice's spine. She wanted to glance around her to see what sort of makeshift weapon she could find, but Liam's gaze was leveled at hers with relentless focus. She tried to remember what might be around her. There was a letter opener over on the desk, but the desk wasn't close and the letter opener would be a sorry match for a gun. So would the fireplace poker, the heavy book Wyatt was reading, and a coffee mug that hadn't yet made it to the dishwasher.

She took another deep, steadying breath. "Did you tell Oscar that Nadia knew? Is he the one who told you that you needed to kill her, too?"

Liam shrugged. "I didn't have to tell him. It was totally obvious to me that I had to kill Nadia. She had my entire future in her hands. Instead of being a well-known pastry chef, I was going to be an inmate. What kind of job would I be able to get after that?"

"Did Oscar tell you why he wanted Arabella dead?"

Liam said impatiently, "Again, he didn't have to. It was totally obvious. Arabella was running her mouth a lot about their partnership. She'd talk to people on the phone about it, telling them that she and Oscar had different visions and it was time for the partnership to split up. It wasn't really a secret. Arabella was dumb to think Oscar didn't know."

"When it came time for Arabella's murder, you decided not to do it, right?"

Liam raised an eyebrow. "How did you figure that out?"

"Well, it was a simple deduction. You'd already put yourself on the line. Maybe Oscar said he wasn't going to pay you more for two murders. Or maybe he thought he needed to off Arabella himself, since you hadn't been able to follow through. She didn't even think he was in town yet—Arabella's housekeeper was busy running errands to prepare for his stay. But Oscar *was* in town, although he claimed he wasn't. This time of year, there are a lot of tourists in downtown Dappled Hills, especially on a weekend. Oscar probably thought he could blend in, follow Arabella, and find an opportunity to murder her. A quiet alley and a set of stairs were the perfect setup."

The front door suddenly burst open, and Meadow stood there, sounding out of breath. "Sorry to drop in! Can I borrow that wrapping paper?" She'd apparently walked over from next door, and had her tremendous dog, Boris, with her, probably letting him stretch his legs while she ran her errands. Then she froze, staring at the scene in front of her: Liam pointing a gun at Beatrice. Noo-noo softly growling and looking pleadingly at Meadow to help fix things.

Liam froze. Then he pointed the gun at Meadow. Then back at Beatrice.

"Seriously?" asked Beatrice. "Are you planning two more murders? They'll lock you up and throw away the key. Liam, think this through."

Boris had *not* frozen. And Boris was not fond of the mood in Beatrice's cottage. He started barking at Liam, showing a lot of very large, sharp teeth. Noo-noo joined in, howling at the end of her barks, showing her very real distress.

Meadow was now turning red in the face. "The very *idea*!"

Liam gestured with the gun. "Get over here. Away from the door. And shut that dog up."

But Boris wouldn't be shut up. He lunged at Liam, then retreated, still snarling. And Liam had apparently had some bad experiences with large dogs at some point in his past. His face was pale, and he backed up slightly, keeping his eyes on Boris.

Which was when Beatrice picked up a large Christmas snow globe and hit Liam over the back of the head with it. He slumped to the floor, out like a light.

Chapter Twenty-One

Meadow stared, her mouth in a big O at Liam on the floor. "We should call Ramsay," said Beatrice in a tired voice. "Do you have your phone?"

But Meadow could do better. She simply stepped outside and hollered, "*Ramsay!*" at the top of her lungs. The poor man was apparently at home eating his dinner . . . a dinner Meadow had, at long last, finally prepared for him.

Minutes later, Ramsay was there. He was breathing hard and still had his napkin tucked into his collar from his time at the dinner table. He stared for a second at Liam, unconscious on the living room floor. "Are you two okay?"

"Thanks to Beatrice," said Meadow. She'd been shaky for the minute or two before Ramsay arrived, but now was in fine fettle and was getting more outraged by the moment. "He was going to *shoot* us, Ramsay! The pastry guy! Shoot us!"

Ramsay felt for Liam's pulse and then, apparently finding it, took out his phone. "Yes, I believe he was. I'll take that gun for safe keeping, please." He reached out his hand to Beatrice, who was holding the pistol she'd taken from Liam after he'd fallen to the floor. She handed it over to him, her hands trembling just a bit.

Ramsay called for an ambulance, then spoke with the state police, asking them to come.

Beatrice said, "You'll need to get Oscar. He might be out of town by now because he was putting things in his trunk earlier. He's the one who planned Arabella's death. And, according to Liam, he was the one who ultimately killed her."

Ramsay quickly related that to the state police, who put out an all-points bulletin. Beatrice described the type of car he was driving. Then, when Ramsay got off the phone, she said, "Is Liam going to be okay?"

"I think he's going to be just fine. He's definitely catching up on some rest now, isn't he?" Ramsay looked at the floor where the massive glass snow globe was resting. Amazingly, it hadn't broken.

The sound of an ambulance siren drew closer. Ramsay put handcuffs on Liam. "The more important question is if the two of *you* are okay." He gave Meadow and Beatrice a serious look as he stood back up.

Meadow's fury was a palpable entity now. "Can you believe it, Ramsay? He was going to murder Beatrice and me. And probably poor Boris and Noo-noo, too."

"Why don't the two of you have a seat?" said Ramsay. He absently bent over to pat Boris, who leaned against him.

Beatrice settled on the sofa and lifted Noo-noo up to join her. The little dog gave her owner a serious look, and Beatrice rubbed her gently. "It's okay," she said to the small dog soothingly.

The ambulance arrived, and the EMTs examined Liam. They checked him for consciousness, breathing, and signs of serious injury. Liam was just waking up, a fact that relieved Beatrice. Despite his intentions toward her, she didn't want to have caused him any permanent harm. The EMTs stabilized his neck and spine as a precaution, then headed out to take him to the hospital. A couple of Ramsay's deputies had arrived on the scene and accompanied Liam in the back of the ambulance.

That done, Ramsay joined Beatrice on the sofa, taking out his ever-present notebook and pencil. Meadow was apparently too strung out to sit down. Instead, she paced around.

"Where's Wyatt? At the church?" asked Ramsay.

"He's visiting a few folks in the hospital," said Beatrice. "He should be coming back home, soon."

"Okay. I'm going to text him to let him know everything is all right over here. I don't want him scared to death when he drives up and sees police cars here." Ramsay lay down his notebook and pencil to send the text, then picked them up again. "Now, let's hear what happened."

Boris, unable to stop himself, gave Ramsay a big, slobbery kiss. Ramsay turned his head to one side, trying unsuccessfully to stop it. "Good boy, good boy," he muttered.

"Boris *is* a good boy," said Beatrice. "He distracted Liam so I could hit him with the snow globe."

"Noo-noo helped too," said Meadow loyally.

Beatrice gave Noo-noo a loving rub. "Yes, she did. It's just that Noo-noo isn't nearly as alarming-looking as Boris when Boris is upset."

"Maybe we should start at the beginning," suggested Ramsay.

Beatrice tried to remember exactly what the beginning was. It had been an endless day. "Well, like I mentioned, I'd seen Oscar outside his hotel, loading his bags in his trunk. I hope you're able to get him."

Ramsay said grimly, "We will, don't worry."

"Anyway, when I was talking to Oscar, I was telling him how nice the funeral reception was. I mentioned that Liam had said he'd spoken to him. But Oscar had told me earlier that he'd never spoken directly to Liam."

Ramsay nodded, making a note in his notebook. "A contradiction, then."

"Exactly. So the next thing I know, I've run my errand and am back home. Noo-noo started whining, and I thought maybe she needed to go out." Beatrice looked rueful. "But I guess she was trying to tell me something else, instead. I just wasn't listening closely enough to her."

Meadow, who'd been muttering angrily to herself as she paced, said, "The poor girl! She was trying to tell you there was a scary man outside the door."

"There was. Liam pushed his way in. I wasn't going to argue with a gun, of course."

Meadow was very indignant. "A gun! In Dappled Hills."

Ramsay shared a look with Beatrice. There were actually plenty of guns in Dappled Hills. Many of them were owned by hunters, since hunting was a popular pastime in the area. And, naturally, Meadow's own husband wore one most of his day. But at this point, Meadow was so completely fired up that she was going to react negatively to anything that was said.

Ramsay said, "So Liam forced his way in with the gun. What happened then?"

"Well, I was trying to buy time. He was threatening both me and Noo-noo, and I just kept thinking if I could keep him talking, maybe someone would show up." Beatrice gave Meadow a grateful look. "And somebody did."

Before Meadow could interject, Ramsay continued quickly, "What was the conversation like between you and Liam?"

"It was mostly me piecing everything together. I told him I knew Oscar had hired Liam to kill Arabella. I figured, like most young people in school, that Liam had plenty of student loan debt. That being offered a good deal of money, even to do something criminal, would be appealing."

Ramsay said, "But Nadia found out about the plan, I'm guessing."

"That's right. Liam thought she overheard him talking on the phone with Oscar because he could tell she looked shocked when he rounded a corner."

"Did Nadia tell him she was going to tell the police?" asked Ramsay.

"That poor girl," muttered Meadow to herself.

"She did. Which was unfortunately a big mistake. I wondered if Nadia was so used to being the authority figure because of the internship that it didn't occur to her that Liam would turn on her."

"Liam's whole future was going to be over," said Ramsay.

"Rightly so," piped up Meadow. She was unsuccessfully trying to calm down Boris, who was still leaping around as if there was something dangerous lurking in the shadows.

Ramsay turned to look at his wife. "Sweetie, why don't you take Boris back home? Give him some treats, since he's such a good boy."

"He *is* a good boy. The best. But I do need that wrapping paper."

Ramsay asked, "Was that the whole reason you and Boris were here?"

"Well, it's a very important reason, after all. I need more wrapping paper. The stores here are closed tomorrow for Christmas Eve, so where was I to go? Boris, of course, doesn't really worry about wrapping paper, but he did need to potty, so I thought I'd kill two birds with one stone." Meadow's face flushed again at the memory of what she'd walked into. "Then, when I came inside, I saw that *monster*."

"Got it," said Ramsay. When Meadow waited, he jotted down notes of what she'd said. "Thank you."

Beatrice said, "If you open the coat closet, Meadow, you'll see a hanging wrapping paper organizer. Take whatever you want."

Meadow reached in, grabbed a roll of Santa paper, then fervently said, "Ramsay, I won't sleep a wink until that Oscar man is in custody."

"We're on it, Meadow."

Meadow bobbed her head, grabbed Boris's leash in one hand, gripped the Santa paper in the other, and walked out. She brandished the wrapping paper in front of her as if ready to take on Oscar if he happened her way.

Ramsay relaxed just a little. "Whew. Bless her. She's even more wound up than she usually is."

"It was a pretty disturbing scene," said Beatrice. "I'll be forever grateful that Meadow pushed her way inside. And that she ran out of wrapping paper in the first place."

"True," said Ramsay. "Okay, where were we? I think you'd just finished explaining why Liam had to murder Nadia. But you were saying he *didn't* murder Arabella? That Oscar had done that?"

"That's what I understand. I guess Oscar felt Liam had botched the whole thing. He wasn't supposed to have murdered Nadia at all. And maybe Oscar felt Liam should have been more circumspect in terms of where he had private, sensitive phone calls. Oscar decided to take on Arabella. He came into town, although he claimed he wasn't in Dappled Hills when Arabella died, followed Arabella, then found an opportunity to push her down the stairs and took it."

Ramsay said, "He didn't have an alibi in Atlanta, which is where he'd said he was when Arabella was murdered. Plus, I'll admit I found Oscar kind of a slippery character. I know he was supposed to be a whiz at administering that big business of theirs, but there was just something about him that seemed really devious to me." He shrugged. "Okay, so you saw Oscar at the hotel. He realized you knew he'd been lying about speaking with Liam. He notified Liam, telling him you were onto them. Then he left town, meaning for Liam to do his dirty work for him."

"Which once again didn't go according to plan," said Beatrice. "But then, Liam was a pastry chef, not a contract killer. At least, he wasn't a contract killer on a regular basis."

The state police had arrived by then. There were a couple outside and an officer who seemed eager to talk with Ramsay.

"Any news?" asked Ramsay.

"We've got him. We've got Oscar Baldwin. Plucked him right off the highway. He's arrested and about to be booked."

Ramsay looked relieved. "Great. Thanks for letting me know."

The police officer walked out, and Ramsay stood up. "Now we can actually spend some time with our families and not worry about a killer on the loose. And Meadow can sleep tonight for once. There's a lot to be thankful for." His phone buzzed, and he checked it. "Looks like Wyatt is on his way back home. You two be sure to take it easy tonight. It's a big day tomorrow."

"Thanks, Ramsay. You try to relax some tonight, too."

Wyatt had come back home just fifteen minutes later. He walked in, spotted Beatrice, and gave her a big, tight hug.

She gave him the story, emphasizing the fact that the bad guys were both in custody. Then she sniffed the air. "What's that I'm smelling?"

Wyatt sniffed. "It smells like something burning."

Beatrice yelped. "My meatloaf!"

Unfortunately, the meatloaf was unredeemable. It resembled a brick instead of the edible substance it was intended to be. Noo-noo looked sorrowfully at the smoky object Beatrice retrieved from the oven.

"I'm so sorry," said Wyatt. "That was really nice of you to cook supper for us."

Beatrice said wryly, "Well, I wanted to. I put it in because I knew you were having a long day and would have an especially long day tomorrow for Christmas Eve."

"And then it ended up that *you* had a long day, too," said Wyatt. He paused. "I'm thinking we order pizza for delivery."

And somehow, it was just as nice to sit in front of the fire, eating a meat-lovers' pizza, and drinking glasses of wine.

The next day was Christmas Eve. It was a busy but special day in the life of the church. So many families reunited with children who'd long left the nest but returned to Dappled Hills and were at church with their parents. Grandparents, grandchildren, and some great-grandchildren squeezed into the pews for the crowded services.

The first service, of course, was the children's service. It was always held at four in the afternoon, a time that seemed to work the best for both naptimes and bedtimes. Although there usually wasn't a sleepy face in the bunch. At this one, Wyatt and Beatrice sat in folding chairs in the family life center with Will, Piper, Ash, Meadow, and Ramsay to watch the Christmas play.

Beatrice had given Edgenora the batteries before the service, without mentioning how the errand had led her to speak with Oscar, which had led to other events. Edgenora was tense, but smiling.

"Remember, the play is going to be just fine," said Beatrice. "The whole cast is adorable, and the audience knows the entire story already, so no one is going to be confused if lines are forgotten. And the costumes look amazing."

Edgenora had brightened at that. "The costumes do look really good."

"Thank goodness you and Savannah and Georgia replaced them. The ones we'd been using for ages looked completely decrepit."

The play had been perfect. The little performers weren't perfect, of course. The angel couldn't remember her lines and hurried to the front of the stage to ask her mother what they were instead of asking Edgenora, who was in the wings for just that eventuality. One member of the children's choir had a terrible case of the hiccups and made the other children giggle. But it put everyone in the room in the Christmas spirit as the tiny Mary and Joseph looked with wide eyes at the infant who was playing the baby Jesus.

Will had been glued to the entire production, taking in the way the "big kids" had represented various characters of the Christmas story. He clapped enthusiastically when the play was over, as did everyone else. Wyatt went up on the stage after the production, thanking all the performers, and asking Edgenora to come out for a bow.

There was another service at eight p.m. in the sanctuary for adults and older children. But Beatrice's favorite was the eleven o'clock service that ended at midnight. It was called the "lessons and carols" service, and featured scripture readings interspersed with Christmas carols. For the last carol, "Silent Night," church elders lit the candles of the members of the congregation at the very ends of the pews. They, in turn, lit the candles of the person next to them until the entire sanctuary was full of candlelight and the overhead lights were dimmed. The congregation sang with the choir and held their candles aloft.

When the service ended at midnight, Wyatt and Beatrice stood at the door, thanking everyone for coming and wishing them Merry Christmas—and it *was* Christmas, just very, very early in the morning.

Christmas morning, Beatrice woke early, a smile on her face from a happy dream that she couldn't seem to remember the details of. She stretched, put on a robe, and then put the breakfast casserole in the oven that she'd put together the day before. They were going to be heading to a proper Christmas feast at Meadow's in an hour or so, but Meadow had requested that Beatrice bring "her famous Christmas breakfast casserole," mostly because it had been traditional when Piper was little. There was not much that was famous about breakfast sausage, white bread, cheese, eggs, milk, and seasonings, but Beatrice thought it was kind of Meadow to ask her to bring it. It did need an hour in the oven, though, so it was good Beatrice had an early start.

Wyatt was up early, too, and was letting Noo-noo out in the front yard. He'd turned on the Christmas tree lights.

"Want to exchange our gifts?" he asked with a smile. "I think our plan was to do that before we headed over to Meadow and Ramsay's house."

"Yes, let's," said Beatrice. "And Noo-noo should get her present, too."

Noo-noo, who'd already eaten her breakfast, still looked very interested in what her present might be. Beatrice looked under the tree, finding a box with Noo-noo's name on it. "Here you are, girl," said Beatrice.

Noo-noo sniffed it curiously, then enthusiastically pushed the top of the box with her nose until the lid came off. Then she pulled out a paper bag of homemade treats Wyatt and Beatrice had bought from a vendor at the craft fair. Wyatt took the bag, opened it, and gave her some of the peanut butter and oat treats, which she happily gobbled up.

Beatrice reached under the tree again, pulling out a thin, wrapped gift for Wyatt. "This is for you."

Wyatt carefully opened it, revealing a vintage vinyl record of jazz musician Miles Davis's "Kind of Blue."

Wyatt's eyes popped when he saw it. "Where did you find this? I've been wanting a vinyl recording for ages. I'd read that this was considered essential for any jazz collection."

Beatrice grinned, pleased that he was excited about the gift. "I drove over to Lenoir one day. I heard the record store there had a nice collection of jazz records. I apparently got lucky, because they said it wasn't usually in stock."

Wyatt gave her a tender kiss. "Should I put it on? I know we should be listening to Christmas music."

"Let's play it. I bet Meadow will have Christmas music playing when we head over there in a little while."

Wyatt carefully took the record out of its sleeve and opened the top of the record player. When he set the needle on the vinyl, the strains of "So What" started playing. Wyatt mentioned how the album was known for its modal jazz style. Beatrice smiled and nodded, although Wyatt had completely lost her. She enjoyed listening to the music more than she enjoyed analyzing it. She was happy he liked her present, though.

Wyatt looked under the Christmas tree for a minute, finally pulling out a box wrapped in red and green striped paper. He handed it gently to Beatrice. "Here you are. Merry Christmas."

She unwrapped the present to find a large glass jar with a decorated lid. Wyatt said shyly, "Meadow helped me decorate the lid. I didn't think I was up to the task."

Beatrice held up the jar, looking inside at all the things on display there. "It's a memory jar," she said slowly. "Oh, it's amazing."

And it was. The jar was filled with mementoes from their year together. She didn't realize Wyatt had been keeping them just for this moment. There were ticket stubs from movies and concerts they'd attended together, pressed flowers from their garden when they were in bloom, candid photographs Beatrice hadn't known Wyatt was taking at family gatherings, fall leaves collected from mountain walks, and bird feathers from a bird-watching outing they'd had.

Wyatt was looking anxiously at her as she took in all the mementoes. "What do you think?"

"I think it's the most thoughtful gift I've ever gotten," said Beatrice honestly.

And although she loved the Christmas chaos at Meadow's house later, the food, Will's wonder, and the laughter with friends and family, nothing matched the next quiet moments on the sofa with just her and Wyatt, holding hands.

About the Author

B estselling cozy mystery author Elizabeth Spann Craig is a library-loving, avid mystery reader. A pet-owning Southerner, her four series are full of cats, corgis, and cheese grits. The mother of two, she lives with her husband, a fun-loving corgi, and a couple of cute cats.

Sign up for Elizabeth's free newsletter to stay updated on releases:

https://bit.ly/2xZUXqO

This and That

I love hearing from my readers. You can find me on Facebook as Elizabeth Spann Craig Author, on Twitter as elizabethscraig, on my website at elizabethspanncraig.com, and by email at elizabethspanncraig@gmail.com.

Thanks so much for reading my book...I appreciate it. If you enjoyed the story, would you please leave a short review on the site where you purchased it? Just a few words would be great. Not only do I feel encouraged reading them, but they also help other readers discover my books. Thank you!

Did you know my books are available in print and ebook formats? Most of the Myrtle Clover series is available in audio and some of the Southern Quilting mysteries are. Find the audiobooks here: https://elizabethspanncraig.com/audio/

Please follow me on BookBub for my reading recommendations and release notifications.

I'd also like to thank some folks who helped me put this book together. Thanks to my cover designer, Karri Klawiter, for her awesome covers. Thanks to my editor, Judy Beatty for her help. Thanks to beta readers Amanda Arrieta, Rebecca Wahr, Cassie Kelley, and Dan Harris for all of their helpful suggestions and careful reading. Thanks to my ARC readers for helping to spread the word. Thanks, as always, to my family and readers.

Other Works by Elizabeth

Myrtle Clover Series in Order (be sure to look for the Myrtle series in audio, ebook, and print):

Pretty is as Pretty Dies
Progressive Dinner Deadly
A Dyeing Shame
A Body in the Backyard
Death at a Drop-In
A Body at Book Club
Death Pays a Visit
A Body at Bunco
Murder on Opening Night
Cruising for Murder
Cooking is Murder
A Body in the Trunk
Cleaning is Murder
Edit to Death
Hushed Up
A Body in the Attic
Murder on the Ballot
Death of a Suitor

A Dash of Murder
Death at a Diner
A Myrtle Clover Christmas
Murder at a Yard Sale
Doom and Bloom
A Toast to Murder
Mystery Loves Company (2025)

THE VILLAGE LIBRARY Mysteries in Order:
Checked Out
Overdue
Borrowed Time
Hush-Hush
Where There's a Will
Frictional Characters
Spine Tingling
A Novel Idea
End of Story
Booked Up
Out of Circulation
Shelf Life (2025)
The Sunset Ridge Mysteries in Order
The Type-A Guide to Solving Murder
The Type-A Guide to Dinner Parties (2025)
Southern Quilting Mysteries in Order:
Quilt or Innocence
Knot What it Seams

Quilt Trip
Shear Trouble
Tying the Knot
Patch of Trouble
Fall to Pieces
Rest in Pieces
On Pins and Needles
Fit to be Tied
Embroidering the Truth
Knot a Clue
Quilt-Ridden
Needled to Death
A Notion to Murder
Crosspatch
Behind the Seams
Quilt Complex
A Southern Quilting Cozy Christmas

MEMPHIS BARBEQUE MYSTERIES in Order (Written as Riley Adams):
Delicious and Suspicious
Finger Lickin' Dead
Hickory Smoked Homicide
Rubbed Out
And a standalone "cozy zombie" novel: Race to Refuge, written as Liz Craig

Printed in the USA
CPSIA information can be obtained
at www.ICGtesting.com
LVHW022244181024
794199LV00002B/428

9 781955 395380